THE DIAMOND AS BIG AS THE RITZ AND OTHER STORIES

BY F. SCOTT FITZGERALD

F. SCOTT FITZGERALD (1896–1940) is best known for his novels and short stories which chronicle the excesses of America's 'Jazz Age' during the 1920s.

Born into a fairly well-to-do family in St Paul, Minnesota, in 1896, Fitzgerald attended, but never graduated from, Princeton University. It was here he mingled with the moneyed classes from the Eastern Seaboard, who were to obsess him for the rest of his life. In 1917 he was drafted into the army, but he never saw active service abroad. Instead, he spent much of his time writing and re-writitng his first novel, *This Side of Paradise*, which on its publication in 1920 was an instant success. In the same year he married the beautiful Zelda Sayre, and together they embarked on a rich life of endless parties. Dividing their time between America and fashionable resorts in Europe, the Fizgeralds became as famous for their lifestyle as for the novels he wrote. Scott Fitzgerald once said 'Sometimes I don't know whether Zelda and I are real or whether we are characters in one of my novels.' He followed his first success with *The Beautiful and the Damned* (1922), and *The Great Gatsby* (1925), which many critics, and Fitzgerald himself, consider his masterpiece. It was also at this time that he wrote many of his short stories, which helped to pay for his extravagant lifestyle.

The bubble burst in the 1930s when Zelda became increasingly troubled by mental illness. *Tender is the Night* (1934), the story of Dick Diver and his schizophrenic wife Nicole, goes some way to show the pain that Fitzgerald felt. The book was not well received in America and he turned to script-writing in Hollywood for the final three years of his life. It was at this time he wrote his autobiographical essays, collected posthumously in *The Crack-Up*, and the unfinished novel *The Last Tycoon*. He died in 1940.

Fitzgerald's short stories are shrewd commentaries on the superficial society of 1920s America and contain some of his most biting satire. This selection includes his most famous and haunting tale, *The Diamond as Big as the Ritz*

PENGUIN POPULAR CLASSICS

THE DIAMOND AS BIG AS THE RITZ AND OTHER STORIES

F. SCOTT FITZGERALD

PENGUIN BOOKS

PENGUIN BOOKS

Published by the Penguin Group
Penguin Books Ltd, 27 Wrights Lane, London w8 5tz, England
Penguin Books USA Inc., 375 Hudson Street, New York, New York 10014, USA
Penguin Books Australia Ltd, Ringwood, Victoria, Australia
Penguin Books Canada Ltd, 10 Alcorn Avenue, Toronto, Ontario, Canada m4v 3b2
Penguin Books (NZ) Ltd, 182–190 Wairau Road, Auckland 10, New Zealand

Penguin Books Ltd, Registered Offices: Harmondsworth, Middlesex, England

This selection first published by The Bodley Head Ltd 1963
Published in Penguin Popular Classics 1996
1 3 5 7 9 10 8 6 4 2

This selection copyright © The Bodley Head Ltd, 1963
All rights reserved

Printed in England by Clays Ltd, St Ives Plc

CONTENTS

THE DIAMOND
AS BIG AS THE RITZ
[1922]

JOHN T. UNGER came from a family that had been well known in Hades—a small town on the Mississippi River—for several generations. John's father had held the amateur golf championship through many a heated contest; Mrs Unger was known 'from hot-box to hot-bed,' as the local phrase went, for her political addresses; and young John T. Unger, who had just turned sixteen, had danced all the latest dances from New York before he put on long trousers. And now, for a certain time, he was to be away from home. That respect for a New England education which is the bane of all provincial places, which drains them yearly of their most promising young men, had seized upon his parents. Nothing would suit them but that he should go to St Midas' School near Boston—Hades was too small to hold their darling and gifted son.

Now in Hades—as you know if you ever have been there—the names of the more fashionable preparatory schools and colleges mean very little. The inhabitants have been so long out of the world that, though they make a show of keeping up to date in dress and manners and literature, they depend to a great extent on hearsay, and a function that in Hades would be considered elaborate would doubt-less be hailed by a Chicago beef-princess as 'perhaps a little tacky.'

John T. Unger was on the eve of departure. Mrs Unger, with maternal fatuity, packed his trunks full of linen suits and electric fans, and Mr Unger presented his son with an asbestos pocket-book stuffed with money.

'Remember, you are always welcome here,' he said. 'You can be sure, boy, that we'll keep the home fires burning.'

'I know,' answered John huskily.

'Don't forget who you are and where you come from,' continued his father proudly, 'and you can do nothing to harm you. You are an Unger—from Hades.'

So the old man and the young shook hands and John walked away with tears streaming from his eyes. Ten minutes later he had passed outside the city limits, and he stopped to glance back for the last time. Over the gates the old-fashioned Victorian motto seemed strangely attractive to him. His father had tried time and time again to have it changed to something with a little more push and verve about it, such as 'Hades—Your Opportunity,' or else a plain 'Welcome' sign set over a hearty handshake pricked out in electric lights. The old motto was a little depressing, Mr Unger had thought—but now . . .

So John took his look and then set his face resolutely towards his destination. And, as he turned away, the lights of Hades against the sky seemed full of a warm and passionate beauty.

St Midas' School is half an hour from Boston in a Rolls-Pierce motor-car. The actual distance will never be known, for no one, except John T. Unger, had ever arrived there save in a Rolls-Pierce and probably no one ever will again. St Midas' is the most expensive and the most exclusive boys' preparatory school in the world.

John's first two years there passed pleasantly. The fathers of all the boys were money-kings and John spent his summers visiting at fashionable resorts. While he was very fond of all the boys he visited, their fathers struck him as being much of a piece, and in his boyish way he often wondered at their exceeding sameness. When he told them where his home was they would ask jovially, 'Pretty hot down there?' and John would muster a faint smile and answer, 'It certainly is.' His response would have been

2*

heartier had they not all made this joke—at best varying it with, 'Is it hot enough for you down there?' which he hated just as much.

In the middle of his second year at school, a quiet, hand-some boy named Percy Washington had been put in John's form. The newcomer was pleasant in his manner and exceedingly well dressed even for St Midas', but for some reason he kept aloof from the other boys. The only person with whom he was intimate was John T. Unger, but even to John he was entirely uncommunicative concerning his home or his family. That he was wealthy went without saying, but beyond a few such deductions John knew little of his friend, so it promised rich confectionery for his curiosity when Percy invited him to spend the summer at his home 'in the West.' He accepted, without hesitation.

It was only when they were in the train that Percy became, for the first time, rather communicative. One day while they were eating lunch in the dining-car and discussing the im-perfect characters of several of the boys at school, Percy suddenly changed his tone and made an abrupt remark.

'My father,' he said, 'is by far the richest man in the world.'

'Oh,' said John, politely. He could think of no answer to make to this confidence. He considered 'That's very nice,' but it sounded hollow and was on the point of saying, 'Really?' but refrained since it would seem to question Percy's statement. And such an astounding statement could scarcely be questioned.

'By far the richest,' repeated Percy.

'I was reading in the *World Almanack*,' began John, 'that there was one man in America with an income of over five million a year and four men with incomes of over three million a year, and——'

'Oh, they're nothing,' Percy's mouth was a half-moon of scorn. 'Catch-penny capitalists, financial small-fry, petty merchants and money-lenders. My father could buy them out and not know he'd done it.'

'But how does he——'

'Why haven't they put down *his* income tax? Because he doesn't pay any. At least he pays a little one—but he doesn't pay any on his *real* income.'

'He must be very rich,' said John simply. 'I'm glad. I like very rich people.'

'The richer a fella is, the better I like him.' There was a look of passionate frankness upon his dark face. 'I visited the Schnlitzer-Murphys last Easter. Vivian Schnlitzer-Murphy had rubies as big as hen's eggs, and sapphires that were like globes with lights inside them——'

'I love jewels,' agreed Percy enthusiastically. 'Of course I wouldn't want anyone at school to know about it, but I've got quite a collection myself. I used to collect them instead of stamps.'

'And diamonds,' continued John eagerly. 'The Schnlitzer-Murphys had diamonds as big as walnuts——'

'That's nothing.' Percy had leaned forward and dropped his voice to a low whisper. 'That's nothing at all. My father has a diamond bigger than the Ritz-Carlton Hotel.'

II

The Montana sunset lay between two mountains like a gigantic bruise from which dark arteries spread themselves over a poisoned sky. An immense distance under the sky crouched the village of Fish, minute, dismal, and forgotten. There were twelve men, so it was said, in the village of Fish, twelve sombre and inexplicable souls who sucked a lean milk from the almost literally bare rock upon which a mysterious populatory force had begotten them. They had become a race apart, these twelve men of Fish, like some species developed by an early whim of nature, which on second thought had abandoned them to struggle and extermination.

Out of the blue-black bruise in the distance crept a long line of moving lights upon the desolation of the land, and the twelve men of Fish gathered like ghosts at the shanty depot to watch the passing of the seven o'clock train, the

Transcontinental Express from Chicago. Six times or so a year the Transcontinental Express, through some inconceivable jurisdiction, stopped at the village of Fish, and when this occurred a figure or so would disembark, mount into a buggy that always appeared from out of the dusk, and drive off towards the bruised sunset. The observation of this pointless and preposterous phenomenon had become a sort of cult among the men of Fish. To observe, that was all; there remained in them none of the vital quality of illusion which would make them wonder or speculate, else a religion might have grown up around these mysterious visitations. But the men of Fish were beyond all religion—the barest and most savage tenets of even Christianity could gain no foothold on that barren rock—so there was no altar, no priest, no sacrifice; only each night at seven the silent concourse by the shanty depot, a congregation who lifted up a prayer of dim, anaemic wonder.

On this June night, the Great Brakeman, whom, had they deified anyone, they might well have chosen as their celestial protagonist, had ordained that the seven o'clock train should leave its human (or inhuman) deposit at Fish. At two minutes after seven Percy Washington and John T. Unger disembarked, hurried past the spellbound, the agape, the fearsome eyes of the twelve men of Fish, mounted into a buggy which had obviously appeared from nowhere, and drove away.

After half an hour, when the twilight had coagulated into dark, the silent negro who was driving the buggy hailed an opaque body somewhere ahead of them in the gloom. In response to his cry, it turned upon them a luminous disk which regarded them like a malignant eye out of the unfathomable night. As they came closer, John saw that it was the tail-light of an immense automobile, larger and more magnificent than any he had ever seen. Its body was of gleaming metal richer than nickel and lighter than silver, and the hubs of the wheels were studded with iridescent geometric figures of green and yellow—John did not dare to guess whether they were glass or jewel.

Two negroes, dressed in glittering livery such as one sees in pictures of royal processions in London, were standing at attention beside the car and as the two young men dismounted from the buggy they were greeted in some language which the guest could not understand, but which seemed to be an extreme form of the Southern negro's dialect.

'Get in,' said Percy to his friend, as their trunks were tossed to the ebony roof of the limousine. 'Sorry we had to bring you this far in that buggy, but of course it wouldn't do for the people on the train or those Godforsaken fellas in Fish to see this automobile.'

'Gosh! What a car!' This ejaculation was provoked by its interior. John saw that the upholstery consisted of a thousand minute and exquisite tapestries of silk, woven with jewels and embroideries, and set upon a background of cloth of gold. The two armchair seats in which the boys luxuriated were covered with stuff that resembled duvetyn, but seemed woven in numberless colours of the ends of ostrich feathers.

'What a car!' cried John again, in amazement.

'This thing?' Percy laughed. 'Why, it's just an old junk we use for a station wagon.'

By this time they were gliding along through the darkness towards the break between the two mountains.

'We'll be there in an hour and a half,' said Percy, looking at the clock. 'I may as well tell you it's not going to be like anything you ever saw before.'

If the car was any indication of what John would see, he was prepared to be astonished indeed. The simple piety prevalent in Hades has the earnest worship of and respect for riches as the first article of its creed—had John felt otherwise than radiantly humble before them, his parents would have turned away in horror at the blasphemy.

They had now reached and were entering the break between the two mountains and almost immediately the way became much rougher.

'If the moon shone down here, you'd see that we're in a

big gulch,' said Percy, trying to peer out of the window. He spoke a few words into the mouthpiece and immediately the footman turned on a searchlight and swept the hillsides with an immense beam.

'Rocky, you see. An ordinary car would be knocked to pieces in half an hour. In fact it'd take a tank to navigate it unless you knew the way. You notice we're going uphill now.'

They were obviously ascending, and within a few minutes the car was crossing a high rise, where they caught a glimpse of a pale moon newly risen in the distance. The car stopped suddenly and several figures took shape out of the dark beside it—these were negroes also. Again the two young men were saluted in the same dimly recognizable dialect; then the negroes set to work and four immense cables dangling from overhead were attached with hooks to the hubs of the great jewelled wheels. At a resounding 'Hey-yah!' John felt the car being lifted slowly from the ground—up and up—clear of the tallest rocks on both sides—then higher, until he could see a wavy, moonlit valley stretched out before him in sharp contrast to the quagmire of rocks that they had just left. Only on one side was there still rock—and then suddenly there was no rock beside them or anywhere around.

It was apparent that they had surmounted some immense knife-blade of stone, projecting perpendicularly into the air. In a moment they were going down again, and finally with a soft bump they were landed upon the smooth earth.

'The worst is over,' said Percy, squinting out the window. 'It's only five miles from here, and our own road—tapestry brick—all the way. This belongs to us. This is where the United States ends, father says.'

'Are we in Canada?'

'We are not. We're in the middle of the Montana Rockies. But you are now on the only five square miles of land in the country that's never been surveyed.'

'Why hasn't it? Did they forget it?'

'No,' said Percy, grinning, 'they tried to do it three

times. The first time my grandfather corrupted a whole department of the State survey; the second time he had the official maps of the United States tinkered with—that held them for fifteen years. The last time was harder. My father fixed it so that their compasses were in the strongest magnetic field ever artificially set up. He had a whole set of surveying instruments made with a slight defection that would allow for this territory not to appear, and he substituted them for the ones that were to be used. Then he had a river deflected and he had what looked like a village built up on its banks—so that they'd see it, and think it was a town ten miles farther up the valley. There's only one thing my father's afraid of,' he concluded, 'only one thing in the world that could be used to find us out.'

'What's that?'

Percy sank his voice to a whisper.

'Aeroplanes,' he breathed. 'We've got half-a-dozen anti-aircraft guns and we've arranged it so far—but there've been a few deaths and a great many prisoners. Not that we mind *that*, you know, father and I, but it upsets mother and the girls, and there's always the chance that some time we won't be able to arrange it.'

Shreds and tatters of chinchilla, courtesy clouds in the green moon's heaven, were passing the green moon like precious Eastern stuffs paraded for the inspection of some Tartar Khan. It seemed to John that it was day, and that he was looking at some lads sailing above him in the air, showering down tracts and patent medicine circulars, with their messages of hope for despairing, rockbound hamlets. It seemed to him that he could see them look down out of the clouds and stare—and stare at whatever there was to stare at in this place whither he was bound—What then? Were they induced to land by some insidious device there to be immured far from patent medicines and from tracts until the judgment day—or, should they fail to fall into the trap, did a quick puff of smoke and the sharp round of a splitting shell bring them drooping to earth—and 'upset' Percy's mother and sisters. John shook his head and the wraith of a hollow laugh issued silently from his parted lips. What desperate transaction lay hidden here? What a moral expedient of a bizarre Crœsus? What terrible and golden mystery? . . .

The chinchilla clouds had drifted past now and outside the Montana night was bright as day. The tapestry brick of the road was smooth to the tread of the great tyres as they rounded a still, moonlit lake; they passed into darkness for a moment, a pine grove, pungent and cool, then they came out into a broad avenue of lawn and John's exclamation of pleasure was simultaneous with Percy's taciturn 'We're home.'

Full in the light of the stars, an exquisite château rose from the borders of the lake, climbed in marble radiance half the height of an adjoining mountain, then melted in grace, in perfect symmetry, in translucent feminine languor, into the massed darkness of a forest of pine. The many towers, the slender tracery of the sloping parapets, the chiselled wonder of a thousand yellow windows with their oblongs and hectagons and triangles of golden light, the shattered softness of the intersecting planes of star-shine and blue shade, all trembled on John's spirit like a chord of music. On one of the towers, the tallest, the blackest at its base, an arrangement of exterior lights at the top made a sort of floating fairyland—and as John gazed up in warm enchantment the faint acciaccare sound of violins drifted down in a rococo harmony that was like nothing he had ever heard before. Then in a moment the car stopped before wide, high marble steps around which the night air was fragrant with a host of flowers. At the top of the steps two great doors swung silently open and amber light flooded out upon the darkness, silhouetting the figure of an exquisite lady with black, high-piled hair, who held out her arms towards them.

'Mother,' Percy was saying, 'this is my friend, John Unger, from Hades.'

Afterwards John remembered that first night as a daze of many colours, of quick sensory impressions, of music soft as a voice in love, and of the beauty of things, lights and shadows, and motions and faces. There was a white-haired man who stood drinking a many-hued cordial from a crystal thimble set on a golden stem. There was a girl with a flowery face, dressed like Titania with braided sapphires in her hair. There was a room where the solid, soft gold of the walls yielded to the pressure of his hand, and a room that was like a platonic conception of the ultimate prison—ceiling, floor, and all, it was lined with an unbroken mass of diamonds, diamonds of every size and shape, until, lit with tall violet lamps in the corners, it dazzled the eyes with a whiteness that could be compared only with itself, beyond human wish or dream.

Through a maze of these rooms the two boys wandered. Sometimes the floor under their feet would flame in brilliant patterns from lighting below, patterns of barbaric clashing colours, of pastel delicacy, of sheer whiteness, or of subtle and intricate mosaic, surely from some mosque on the Adriatic Sea. Sometimes beneath layers of thick crystal he would see blue or green water swirling, inhabited by vivid fish and growths of rainbow foliage. Then they would be treading on furs of every texture and colour or along corridors of palest ivory, unbroken as though carved complete from the gigantic tusks of dinosaurs extinct before the age of man. . . .

Then a hazily remembered transition, and they were at dinner—where each plate was of two almost imperceptible layers of solid diamond between which was curiously worked a filigree of emerald design, a shaving sliced from green air. Music, plangent and unobtrusive, drifted down through far corridors—his chair, feathered and curved insidiously to his back, seemed to engulf and overpower him as he drank his first glass of port. He tried drowsily to answer a question that had been asked him, but the honeyed luxury that clasped his body added to the illusion of sleep—jewels, fabrics, wines, and metals blurred before his eyes into a sweet mist. . . .

'Yes,' he replied with a polite effort, 'it certainly is hot enough for me down there.'

He managed to add a ghostly laugh; then, without movement, without resistance, he seemed to float off and away,
leaving an iced dessert that was pink as a dream. . . . He fell
asleep.

When he awoke he knew that several hours had passed.
He was in a great quiet room with ebony walls and a dull
illumination that was too faint, too subtle, to be called a
light. His young host was standing over him.

'You fell asleep at dinner,' Percy was saying. 'I nearly
did, too—it was such a treat to be comfortable again after
this year of school. Servants undressed and bathed you
while you were sleeping.'

'Is this a bed or a cloud?' sighed John. 'Percy, Percy—
before you go, I want to apologize.'

'For what?'

'For doubting you when you said you had a diamond as
big as the Ritz-Carlton hotel.'

Percy smiled.

'I thought you didn't believe me. It's that mountain
you know.'

'What mountain?'

'The mountain the château rests on. It's not very
big for a mountain. But except about fifty feet of sod
and gravel on top it's solid diamond. *One* diamond,
one cubic mile without a flaw. Aren't you listening?
Say——'

But John T. Unger had again fallen asleep.

III

Morning. As he awoke he perceived drowsily that the room
had at the same moment become dense with sunlight. The
ebony panels of one wall had slid aside on a sort of track,
leaving his chamber half open to the day. A large negro in
a white uniform stood beside his bed.

'Good evening,' muttered John, summoning his brains
from the wild places.

'Good morning, sir. Are you ready for your bath, sir?

Oh, don't get up—I'll put you in, if you'll just unbutton your pyjamas—there. Thank you, sir.'

John lay quietly as his pyjamas were removed—he was amused and delighted; he expected to be lifted like a child by this black Gargantua who was tending him, but nothing of the sort happened; instead he felt the bed tilt up slowly on its side—he began to roll, startled at first, in the direction of the wall, but when he reached the wall its drapery gave way, and sliding two yards farther down a fleecy incline he plumped gently into water the same temperature as his body.

He looked about him. The runway or rollway on which he had arrived had folded gently back into place. He had been projected into another chamber and was sitting in a sunken bath with his head just above the level of the floor. All about him, lining the walls of the room and the sides and bottom of the bath itself, was a blue aquarium, and gazing through the crystal surface on which he sat, he could see fish swimming among amber lights and even gliding without curiosity past his outstretched toes, which were separated from them only by the thickness of the crystal. From overhead, sunlight came down through sea-green glass.

'I suppose, sir, that you'd like hot rosewater and soapsuds this morning, sir—and perhaps cold salt water to finish.'

The negro was standing beside him.

'Yes,' agreed John, smiling inanely, 'as you please.' Any idea of ordering this bath according to his own meagre standards of living would have been priggish and not a little wicked.

The negro pressed a button and a warm rain began to fall, apparently from overhead, but really, so John discovered after a moment, from a fountain arrangement near by. The water turned to a pale rose colour and jets of liquid soap spurted into it from four miniature walrus heads at the corners of the bath. In a moment a dozen little paddle-wheels, fixed to the sides, had churned the mixture into a radiant rainbow of pink foam which enveloped him softly with its delicious lightness, and burst in shining, rosy bubbles here and there about him.

'Shall I turn on the moving-picture machine, sir?' suggested the negro deferentially. 'There's a good one-reel comedy in this machine to-day, or I can put in a serious piece in a moment, if you prefer it.'

'No, thanks,' answered John, politely but firmly. He was enjoying his bath too much to desire any distraction. But distraction came. In a moment he was listening intently to the sound of flutes from just outside, flutes dripping a melody that was like a waterfall, cool and green as the room itself, accompanying a frothy piccolo, in play more fragile than the lace of suds that covered and charmed him.

After a cold salt-water bracer and a cold fresh finish, he stepped out and into a fleecy robe, and upon a couch covered with the same material he was rubbed with oil, alcohol, and spice. Later he sat in a voluptuous chair while he was shaved and his hair was trimmed.

'Mr Percy is waiting in your sitting-room,' said the negro, when these operations were finished. 'My name is Gygsum, Mr Unger, sir. I am to see to Mr Unger every morning.'

John walked out into the brisk sunshine of his living-room, where he found breakfast waiting for him and Percy, gorgeous in white kid knickerbockers, smoking in an easy chair.

IV

This is a story of the Washington family as Percy sketched it for John during breakfast.

The father of the present Mr Washington had been a Virginian, a direct descendant of George Washington, and Lord Baltimore. At the close of the Civil War he was a twenty-five-year-old Colonel with a played-out plantation and about a thousand dollars in gold.

Fitz-Norman Culpepper Washington, for that was the

young Colonel's name, decided to present the Virginia estate to his younger brother and go West. He selected two dozen of the most faithful blacks, who, of course, worshipped him, and bought twenty-five tickets to the West, where he intended to take out land in their names and start a sheep and cattle ranch.

When he had been in Montana for less than a month and things were going very poorly indeed, he stumbled on his great discovery. He had lost his way when riding in the hills, and after a day without food he began to grow hungry. As he was without his rifle, he was forced to pursue a squirrel, and in the course of the pursuit he noticed that it was carrying something shiny in its mouth. Just before it vanished into its hole—for Providence did not intend that this squirrel should alleviate his hunger—it dropped its burden. Sitting down to consider the situation Fitz-Norman's eye was caught by a gleam in the grass beside him. In ten seconds he had completely lost his appetite and gained one hundred thousand dollars. The squirrel which had refused with annoying persistence to become food, had made him a present of a large and perfect diamond.

Late that night he found his way to camp and twelve hours later all the males among his darkies were back by the squirrel hole digging furiously at the side of the mountain. He told them he had discovered a rhinestone mine, and, as only one or two of them had ever seen even a small diamond before, they believed him, without question. When the magnitude of his discovery became apparent to him, he found himself in a quandary. The mountain was *a* diamond —it was literally nothing else but solid diamond. He filled four saddle bags full of glittering samples and started on horseback for St Paul. There he managed to dispose of half a dozen small stones—when he tried a larger one a storekeeper fainted and Fitz-Norman was arrested as a public disturber. He escaped from jail and caught the train for New York, where he sold a few medium-sized diamonds and received in exchange about two hundred thousand dollars in gold. But he did not dare to produce any exceptional gems—in fact, he left New York just in time. Tremendous excitement had been created in jewellery circles, not so much by the size of his diamonds as by their appearance in the city from mysterious sources. Wild rumours became current that a diamond mine had been discovered in the Catskills, on the Jersey coast, on Long Island, beneath Washington Square. Excursion trains, packed with men carrying picks and shovels, began to leave New York hourly, bound for various neighbouring El Dorados. But by that time young Fitz-Norman was on his way back to Montana.

By the end of a fortnight he had estimated that the ıamond in the mountain was approximately equal in quantity to all the rest of the diamonds known to exist in the world. There was no valuing it by any regular computation, however, for it was *one solid diamond*—and if it were offered for sale not only would the bottom fall out of the market, but also, if the value should vary with its size in the usual arithmetical progression, there would not be enough gold in the world to buy a tenth part of it. And what could anyone do with a diamond that size?

It was an amazing predicament. He was, in one sense, the richest man that ever lived—and yet was he worth anything at all? If his secret should transpire there was no telling to what measures the Government might resort in order to prevent a panic, in gold as well as in jewels. They might take over the claim immediately and institute a monopoly.

There was no alternative—he must market his mountain in secret. He sent South for his younger brother and put him in charge of his coloured following—darkies who had never realized that slavery was abolished. To make sure of this, he read them a proclamation that he had composed, which announced that General Forrest had reorganized the shattered Southern armies and defeated the North in one pitched battle. The negroes believed him implicitly. They passed a vote declaring it a good thing and held revival services immediately.

Fitz-Norman himself set out for foreign parts with one

hundred thousand dollars and two trunks filled with rough
diamonds of all sizes. He sailed for Russia in a Chinese junk
and six months after his departure from Montana he was in
St Petersburg. He took obscure lodgings and called immediately upon the court jeweller, announcing that he had
a diamond for the Czar. He remained in St Petersburg for
two weeks, in constant danger of being murdered, living
from lodging to lodging, and afraid to visit his trunks more
than three or four times during the whole fortnight.

On his promise to return in a year with larger and finer
stones, he was allowed to leave for India. Before he left,
however, the Court Treasurers had deposited to his credit,
in American banks, the sum of fifteen million dollars—under
four different aliases.

He returned to America in 1868, having been gone a little
over two years. He had visited the capitals of twenty-two
countries and talked with five emperors, eleven kings, three
princes, a shah, a khan, and a sultan. At that time, Fitz-
Norman estimated his own wealth at one billion dollars.
One fact worked consistently against the disclosure of his
secret. No one of his larger diamonds remained in the public
eye for a week before being invested with a history of enough
fatalities, amours, revolutions and wars to have occupied it
from the days of the first Babylonian Empire.

From 1870 until his death in 1900, the history of Fitz-
Norman Washington was a long epic in gold. There were
side issues, of course—he evaded the surveys, he married a
Virginia lady, by whom he had a single son, and he was
compelled, due to a series of unfortunate complications, to
murder his brother, whose unfortunate habit of drinking
himself into an indiscreet stupor had several times en-
dangered their safety. But very few other murders stained
these happy years of progress and expansion.

Just before he died he changed his policy, and with all
but a few million dollars of his outside wealth bought up
rare minerals in bulk, which he deposited in the safety vaults
of banks all over the world, marked as bric-a-brac. His son,
Braddock Tarleton Washington, followed this policy on an

even more intensive scale. The minerals were converted into the rarest of all elements—radium—so that the equivalent of a billion dollars in gold could be placed in a receptacle no bigger than a cigar box.

When Fitz-Norman had been dead three years his son, Braddock, decided that the business had gone far enough. The amount of wealth that he and his father had taken out of the mountain was beyond all exact computation. He kept a note-book in cipher in which he set down the approximate quantity of radium in each of the thousand banks he patronized, and recorded the alias under which it was held. Then he did a very simple thing—he sealed up the mine.

He sealed up the mine. What had been taken out of it would support all the Washingtons yet to be born in unparalleled luxury for generations. His one care must be the protection of his secret, lest in the possible panic attendant on its discovery he should be reduced with all the property-holders in the world to utter poverty.

This was the family among whom John T. Unger was staying. This was the story he heard in his silver-walled living-room the morning after his arrival.

V

After breakfast, John found his way out the great marble entrance, and looked curiously at the scene before him. The whole valley, from the diamond mountain to the steep granite cliff five miles away, still gave off a breath of golden haze which hovered idly above the fine sweep of lawns and lakes and gardens. Here and there clusters of elms made delicate groves of shade, contrasting strangely with the tough masses of pine forest that held the hills in a grip of dark-blue green. Even as John looked he saw three fawns in single file patter out from one clump about a half mile away and disappear with awkward gaiety into the black-ribbed half-light of another. John would not have been surprised to see a goat foot-piping his way among the trees or to catch a glimpse of pink nymph-skin and flying yellow hair between the greenest of the green leaves.

In some such cool hope he descended the marble steps, disturbing faintly the sleep of two silky Russian wolfhounds at the bottom, and set off along a walk of white and blue brick that seemed to lead in no particular direction.

He was enjoying himself as much as he was able. It is youth's felicity as well as its insufficiency that it can never live in the present, but must always be measuring up the day against its own radiantly imagined future—flowers and gold, girls and stars, they are only pre-figurations and prophecies of that incomparable, unattainable young dream.

John rounded a soft corner where the massed rosebushes filled the air with heavy scent, and struck off across a park towards a patch of moss under some trees. He had never lain upon moss, and he wanted to see whether it was really soft enough to justify the use of its name as an adjective. Then he saw a girl coming towards him over the grass. She was the most beautiful person he had ever seen.

She was dressed in a white little gown that came just below her knees, and a wreath of mignonettes clasped with blue slices of sapphire bound up her hair. Her pink bare feet scattered the dew before them as she came. She was younger than John—not more than sixteen.

'Hello,' she cried softly, 'I'm Kismine.'

She was much more than that to John already. He advanced towards her, scarcely moving as he drew near lest he should tread on her bare toes.

'You haven't met me,' said her soft voice. Her blue eyes added, 'Oh, but you've missed a great deal!' . . . 'You met my sister, Jasmine, last night. I was sick with lettuce poisoning,' went on her soft voice, and her eyes continued, 'and when I'm sick I'm sweet—and when I'm well.'

'You have made an enormous impression on me,' said John's eyes, 'and I'm not so slow myself'—'How do you do?' said his voice. 'I hope you're better this morning.' 'You darling,' added his eyes tremulously.

John observed that they had been walking along the path.

On her suggestion they sat down together upon the moss, the softness of which he failed to determine.

He was critical about women. A single defect—a thick ankle, a hoarse voice, a glass eye—was enough to make him utterly indifferent. And here for the first time in his life he was beside a girl who seemed to him the incarnation of physical perfection.

'Are you from the East?' asked Kismine with charming interest.

'No,' answered John simply. 'I'm from Hades.'

Either she had never heard of Hades, or she could think of no pleasant comment to make upon it, for she did not discuss it further.

'I'm going East to school this fall,' she said. 'D'you think I'll like it? I'm going to New York to Miss Bulge's. It's very strict, but you see over the weekends I'm going to live at home with the family in our New York house, because father heard that the girls had to go walking two by two.'

'Your father wants you to be proud,' observed John.

'We are,' she answered, her eyes shining with dignity. 'None of us has ever been punished. Father said we never should be. Once when my sister Jasmine was a little girl she pushed him downstairs and he just got up and limped away.

'Mother was—well, a little startled,' continued Kismine, 'when she heard that you were from—from where you *are* from, you know. She said that when she was a young girl—but then, you see, she's a Spaniard and old-fashioned.'

'Do you spend much time out here?' asked John, to conceal the fact that he was somewhat hurt by this remark. It seemed an unkind allusion to his provincialism.

'Percy and Jasmine and I are here every summer, but next summer Jasmine is going to Newport. She's coming out in London a year from this fall. She'll be presented at Court.'

'Do you know,' began John hesitantly, 'you're much more sophisticated than I thought you were when I first saw you?'

'Oh, no, I'm not,' she exclaimed hurriedly. 'Oh, I

wouldn't think of being. I think that sophisticated young people are *terribly* common, don't you? I'm not at all, really. If you say I am, I'm going to cry.'

She was so distressed that her lip was trembling. John was impelled to protest:

'I didn't mean that; I only said it to tease you.'

'Because I wouldn't mind if I *were*,' she persisted, 'but I'm *not*. I'm very innocent and girlish. I never smoke, or drink, or read anything except poetry. I know scarcely any mathematics or chemistry. I dress *very* simply—in fact, I scarcely dress at all. I think sophisticated is the last thing you can say about me. I believe that girls ought to enjoy their youths in a wholesome way.'

'I do too,' said John heartily.

Kismine was cheerful again. She smiled at him, and a still-born tear dripped from the corner of one blue eye.

'I like you,' she whispered, intimately. 'Are you going to spend all your time with Percy while you're here, or will you be nice to me? Just think—I'm absolutely fresh ground. I've never had a boy in love with me in all my life. I've never been allowed even to *see* boys alone—except Percy. I came all the way out here into this grove hoping to run into you, where the family wouldn't be around.'

Deeply flattered, John bowed from the hips as he had been taught at dancing school in Hades.

'We'd better go now,' said Kismine sweetly. 'I have to be with mother at eleven. You haven't asked me to kiss you once. I thought boys always did that nowadays.'

John drew himself up proudly.

'Some of them do,' he answered, 'but not me. Girls don't do that sort of thing—in Hades.'

Side by side they walked back towards the house.

VI

John stood facing Mr Braddock Washington in the full sunlight. The elder man was about forty with a proud, vacuous face, intelligent eyes, and a robust figure. In the mornings he smelt of horses—the best horses. He carried a plain walking-stick of grey birch with a single large opal for a grip. He and Percy were showing John around.

'The slaves' quarters are there.' His walking-stick indicated a cloister of marble on their left that ran in graceful Gothic along the side of the mountain. 'In my youth I was distracted for a while from the business of life by a period of absurd idealism. During that time they lived in luxury. For instance, I equipped every one of their rooms with a tile bath.'

'I suppose,' ventured John, with an ingratiating laugh, 'that they used the bathtubs to keep coal in. Mr Schnlitzer-Murphy told me that once he——'

'The opinions of Mr Schnlitzer-Murphy are of little importance, I should imagine,' interrupted Braddock Washington, coldly. 'My slaves did not keep coal in their bathtubs. They had orders to bathe every day, and they did. If they hadn't I might have ordered a sulphuric acid shampoo. I discontinued the baths for quite another reason. Several of them caught cold and died. Water is not good for certain races—except as a beverage.'

John laughed, and then decided to nod his head in sober agreement. Braddock Washington made him uncomfortable.

'All these negroes are descendants of the ones my father brought North with him. There are about two hundred and fifty now. You notice that they've lived so long apart from the world that their original dialect has become an almost indistinguishable patois. We bring a few of them up to speak English—my secretary and two or three of the house servants.

'This is the golf course,' he continued, as they strolled along the velvet winter grass. 'It's all a green, you see—no fairway, no rough, no hazards.'

He smiled pleasantly at John.

'Many men in the cage, father?' asked Percy suddenly.

Braddock Washington stumbled, and let forth an involuntary curse.

'One less than there should be,' he ejaculated darkly—

and then added after a moment, 'We've had difficulties.'

'Mother was telling me,' exclaimed Percy, 'that Italian teacher——'

'A ghastly error,' said Braddock Washington angrily. 'But of course there's a good chance that we may have got him. Perhaps he fell somewhere in the woods or stumbled over a cliff. And then there's always the probability that if he did get away his story wouldn't be believed. Nevertheless, I've had two dozen men looking for him in different towns around here.'

'And no luck?'

'Some. Fourteen of them reported to my agent that they'd each killed a man answering to that description, but of course it was probably only the reward they were after——'

He broke off. They had come to a large cavity in the earth about the circumference of a merry-go-round and covered by a strong iron grating. Braddock Washington beckoned to John, and pointed his cane down through the grating. John stepped to the edge and gazed. Immediately his ears were assailed by a wild clamour from below.

'Come on down to Hell!'

'Hello, kiddo, how's the air up there?'

'Hey! Throw us a rope!'

'Got an old doughnut, Buddy, or a couple of second-hand sandwiches?'

'Say, fella, if you'll push down that guy you're with, we'll show you a quick disappearance scene.'

'Paste him one for me, will you?'

It was too dark to see clearly into the pit below, but John could tell from the coarse optimism and rugged vitality of the remarks and voices that they proceeded from middle-class Americans of the more spirited type. Then Mr Washington put out his cane and touched a button in the grass, and the scene below sprang into light.

'These are some adventurous mariners who had the misfortune to discover El Dorado,' he remarked.

Below them there had appeared a large hollow in the earth shaped like the interior of a bowl. The sides were steep and apparently of polished glass, and on its slightly concave surface stood about two dozen men clad in the half costume, half uniform, of aviators. Their upturned faces, lit with wrath, with malice, with despair, with cynical humour, were covered by long growths of beard, but with the exception of a few who had pined perceptibly away, they seemed to be a well-fed, healthy lot.

Braddock Washington drew a garden chair to the edge of the pit and sat down.

'Well, how are you, boys?' he inquired genially.

A chorus of execration in which all joined except a few too dispirited to cry out, rose up into the sunny air, but Braddock Washington heard it with unruffled composure. When its last echo had died away he spoke again.

'Have you thought up a way out of your difficulty?'

From here and there among them a remark floated up.

'We decided to stay here for love!'

'Bring us up there and we'll find us a way!'

Braddock Washington waited until they were again quiet. Then he said:

'I've told you the situation. I don't want you here. I wish to heaven I'd never seen you. Your own curiosity got you here, and any time that you can think of a way out which protects me and my interests I'll be glad to consider it. But so long as you confine your efforts to digging tunnels— yes, I know about the new one you've started—you won't get very far. This isn't as hard on you as you make it out, with all your howling for the loved ones at home. If you were the type who worried much about the loved ones at home, you'd never have taken up aviation.'

A tall man moved apart from the others, and held up his hand to call his captor's attention to what he was about to say.

'Let me ask you a few questions!' he cried. 'You pretend to be a fair-minded man.'

'How absurd. How could a man of *my* position be fair-minded towards *you*? You might as well speak of a Spaniard being fair-minded towards a piece of steak.'

At this harsh observation the faces of the two dozen steaks fell, but the tall man continued:

'All right!' he cried. 'We've argued this out before. You're not a humanitarian and you're not fair-minded, but you're human—at least you say you are—and you ought to be able to put yourself in our place for long enough to think how—how—how——'

'How what?' demanded Washington, coldly.

'—how unnecessary——'

'Not to me.'

'Well,—how cruel——'

'We've covered that. Cruelty doesn't exist where self-preservation is involved. You've been soldiers: you know that. Try another.'

'Well, then, how stupid.'

'There,' admitted Washington, 'I grant you that. But try to think of an alternative. I've offered to have all or any of you painlessly executed if you wish. I've offered to have your wives, sweethearts, children, and mothers kidnapped and brought out here. I'll enlarge your place down there and feed and clothe you the rest of your lives. If there was some method of producing permanent amnesia I'd have all of you operated on and released immediately, somewhere outside of my preserves. But that's as far as my ideas go.'

'How about trusting us not to peach on you?' cried someone.

'You don't proffer that suggestion seriously,' said Washington, with an expression of scorn. 'I did take out one man to teach my daughter Italian. Last week he got away.'

A wild yell of jubilation went up suddenly from two dozen throats and a pandemonium of joy ensued. The prisoners clog-danced and cheered and yodelled and wrestled with one another in a sudden uprush of animal spirits. They even ran up the glass sides of the bowl as far as they could, and slid back to the bottom upon the natural cushions of their bodies. The tall man started a song in which they all joined——

> '*Oh, we'll hang the kaiser*
> *On a sour apple tree——*'

Braddock Washington sat in inscrutable silence until the song was over.

'You see,' he remarked, when he could gain a modicum of attention. 'I bear you no ill-will. I like to see you enjoying yourselves. That's why I didn't tell you the whole story at once. The man—what was his name? Critchtichiello?—was shot by some of my agents in fourteen different places.'

Not guessing that the places referred to were cities, the tumult of rejoicing subsided immediately.

'Nevertheless,' cried Washington with a touch of anger, 'he tried to run away. Do you expect me to take chances with any of you after an experience like that?'

Again a series of ejaculations went up.

'Sure!'

'Would your daughter like to learn Chinese?'

'Hey, I can speak Italian! My mother was a wop.'

'Maybe she'd like t'learna speak N'Yawk!'

'If she's the little one with the big blue eyes I can teach her a lot of things better than Italian.'

'I know some Irish songs—and I could hammer brass once't.'

Mr Washington reached forward suddenly with his cane and pushed the button in the grass so that the picture below went out instantly, and there remained only that great dark mouth covered dismally with the black teeth of the grating.

'Hey!' called a single voice from below, 'you ain't goin' away without givin' us your blessing?'

But Mr Washington, followed by the two boys, was already strolling on towards the ninth hole of the golf course, as though the pit and its contents were no more than a hazard over which his facile iron had triumphed with ease.

VII

July under the lee of the diamond mountain was a month of blanket nights and of warm, glowing days. John and Kismine were in love. He did not know that the little gold football (inscribed with the legend *Pro deo et patria et St*

Mida) which he had given her rested on a platinum chain next to her bosom. But it did. And she for her part was not aware that a large sapphire which had dropped one day from her simple coiffure was stowed away tenderly in John's jewel box.

Late one afternoon when the ruby and ermine music room was quiet, they spent an hour there together. He held her hand and she gave him such a look that he whispered her name aloud. She bent towards him—then hesitated.

'Did you say "Kismine"?' she asked softly, 'or——'

She had wanted to be sure. She thought she might have misunderstood.

Neither of them had ever kissed before, but in the course of an hour it seemed to make little difference.

The afternoon drifted away. That night when a last breath of music drifted down from the highest tower, they each lay awake, happily dreaming over the separate minutes of the day. They had decided to be married as soon as possible.

VIII

Every day Mr Washington and the two young men went hunting or fishing in the deep forests or played golf around the somnolent course—games which John diplomatically allowed his host to win—or swam in the mountain coolness of the lake. John found Mr Washington a somewhat exacting personality—utterly uninterested in any ideas or opinions except his own. Mrs Washington was aloof and reserved at all times. She was apparently indifferent to her two daughters, and entirely absorbed in her son Percy, with whom she held interminable conversations in rapid Spanish at dinner.

Jasmine, the elder daughter, resembled Kismine in appearance—except that she was somewhat bow-legged, and terminated in large hands and feet—but was utterly unlike her in temperament. Her favourite books had to do with poor girls who kept house for widowed fathers. John learned from Kismine that Jasmine had never recovered from the shock and disappointment caused her by the termination of the World War, just as she was about to start for Europe as a canteen expert. She had even pined away for a time, and Braddock Washington had taken steps to promote a new war in the Balkans—but she had seen a photograph of some wounded Serbian soldiers and lost interest in the whole proceedings. But Percy and Kismine seemed to have inherited the arrogant attitude in all its harsh magnificence from their father. A chaste and consistent selfishness ran like a pattern through their every idea.

John was enchanted by the wonders of the château and the valley. Braddock Washington, so Percy told him, had caused to be kidnapped a landscape gardener, an architect, a designer of stage settings, and a French decadent poet left over from the last century. He had put his entire force of negroes at their disposal, guaranteed to supply them with any materials that the world could offer, and left them to work out some ideas of their own. But one by one they had shown their uselessness. The decadent poet had at once begun bewailing his separation from the boulevards in spring—he made some vague remarks about spices, apes, and ivories, but said nothing that was of any practical value. The stage designer on his part wanted to make the whole valley a series of tricks and sensational effects—a state of things that the Washingtons would soon have grown tired of. And as for the architect and the landscape gardener, they thought only in terms of convention. They must make this like this and that like that.

But they had, at least, solved the problem of what was to be done with them—they all went mad early one morning after spending the night in a single room trying to agree upon the location of a fountain, and were now confined comfortably in an insane asylum at Westport, Connecticut.

'But,' inquired John curiously, 'who did plan all your wonderful reception rooms and halls, and approaches and bathrooms——?'

'Well,' answered Percy, 'I blush to tell you, but it was a moving-picture fella. He was the only man we found who was used to playing with an unlimited amount of money, though he did tuck his napkin in his collar and couldn't read or write.'

As August drew to a close John began to regret that he must soon go back to school. He and Kismine had decided to elope the following June.

'It would be nicer to be married here,' Kismine confessed, 'but of course I could never get father's permission to marry you at all. Next to that I'd rather elope. It's terrible for wealthy people to be married in America at present— they always have to send out bulletins to the press saying that they're going to be married in remnants, when what they mean is just a peck of old second-hand pearls and some used lace worn once by the Empress Eugénie.'

'I know,' agreed John fervently. 'When I was visiting the Schnlitzer-Murphys, the eldest daughter, Gwendolyn, married a man whose father owns half of West Virginia. She wrote home saying what a tough struggle she was carrying on on his salary as a bank clerk—and then she ended up by saying that "Thank God, I have four good maids anynow, and that helps a little."'

'It's absurd,' commented Kismine. 'Think of the millions and millions of people in the world, labourers and all, who get along with only two maids.'

One afternoon late in August a chance remark of Kismine's changed the face of the entire situation, and threw John into a state of terror.

They were in their favourite grove, and between kisses John was indulging in some romantic forebodings which he fancied added poignancy to their relations.

'Sometimes I think we'll never marry,' he said sadly. 'You're too wealthy, too magnificent. No one as rich as you are can be like other girls. I should marry the daughter of some well-to-do wholesale hardware man from Omaha or Sioux City, and be content with her half-million.'

'I knew the daughter of a wholesale hardware man once,' remarked Kismine 'I don't think you'd have been contented with her. She was a friend of my sister's. She visited here.'

'Oh, then you've had other guests?' exclaimed John in surprise.

Kismine seemed to regret her words.

'Oh, yes,' she said hurriedly, 'we've had a few.'

'But aren't you—wasn't your father afraid they'd talk outside?'

'Oh, to some extent, to some extent,' she answered. 'Let's talk about something pleasanter.'

But John's curiosity was aroused.

'Something pleasanter!' he demanded. 'What's unpleasant about that? Weren't they nice girls?'

To his great surprise Kismine began to weep.

'Yes—th—that's the—the whole t-trouble. I grew qu-quite attached to some of them. So did Jasmine, but she kept inv-viting them anyway. I couldn't under*stand* it.'

A dark suspicion was born in John's heart.

'Do you mean that they *told*, and your father had them —removed?'

'Worse than that,' she muttered brokenly. 'Father took no chances—and Jasmine kept writing them to come, and they had *such* a good time!'

She was overcome by a paroxysm of grief.

Stunned with the horror of this revelation, John sat there open-mouthed, feeling the nerves of his body twitter like so many sparrows perched upon his spinal column.

'Now, I've told you, and I shouldn't have,' she said, calming suddenly and drying her dark blue eyes.

'Do you mean to say that your father had them *murdered* before they left?'

She nodded.

'In August usually—or early in September. It's only natural for us to get all the pleasure out of them that we can first.'

'How abominable! How—why, I must be going crazy! Did you really admit that——'

'I did,' interrupted Kismine, shrugging her shoulders.

'We can't very well imprison them like those aviators, where they'd be a continual reproach to us every day. And it's always been made easier for Jasmine and me, because father had it done sooner than we expected. In that way we avoided any farewell scene——'

'So you murdered them! Uh!' cried John.

'It was done very nicely. They were drugged while they were asleep—and their families were always told that they died of scarlet fever in Butte.'

'But—I fail to understand why you kept on inviting them!'

'I didn't,' burst out Kismine. 'I never invited one. Jasmine did. And they always had a very good time. She'd give them the nicest presents towards the last. I shall probably have visitors too—I'll harden up to it. We can't let such an inevitable thing as death stand in the way of enjoying life while we have it. Think how lonesome it'd be out here if we never had *any* one. Why, father and mother have sacrificed some of their best friends just as we have.'

'And so,' cried John accusingly, 'and so you were letting me make love to you and pretending to return it, and talking about marriage, all the time knowing perfectly well that I'd never get out of here alive——'

'No,' she protested passionately. 'Not any more. I did at first. You were here. I couldn't help that, and I thought your last days might as well be pleasant for both of us. But then I fell in love with you, and—and I'm honestly sorry you're going to—going to be put away—though I'd rather you'd be put away than ever kiss another girl.'

'Oh, you would, would you?' cried John ferociously.

'Much rather. Besides, I've always heard that a girl can have more fun with a man whom she knows she can never marry. Oh, why did I tell you? I've probably spoiled your whole good time now, and we were really enjoying things when you didn't know it. I knew it would make things sort of depressing for you.'

'Oh, you did, did you?' John's voice trembled with anger. 'I've heard about enough of this. If you haven't any more pride and decency than to have an affair with a fellow that you know isn't much better than a corpse, I don't want to have any more to do with you!'

'You're not a corpse!' she protested in horror. 'You're not a corpse! I won't have you saying that I kissed a corpse!'

'I said nothing of the sort!'

'You did! You said I kissed a corpse!'

'I didn't!'

Their voices had risen, but upon a sudden interruption they both subsided into immediate silence. Footsteps were coming along the path in their direction, and a moment later the rose bushes were parted displaying Braddock Washington, whose intelligent eyes set in his good-looking vacuous face were peering in at them.

'Who kissed a corpse?' he demanded in obvious disapproval.

'Nobody,' answered Kismine quickly. 'We were just joking.'

'What are you two doing here, anyhow?' he demanded gruffly. 'Kismine, you ought to be—to be reading or playing golf with your sister. Go read! Go play golf! Don't let me find you here when I come back!'

Then he bowed at John and went up the path.

'See?' said Kismine crossly, when he was out of hearing. 'You've spoiled it all. We can never meet any more. He won't let me meet you. He'd have you poisoned if he thought we were in love.'

'We're not, any more!' cried John fiercely, 'so he can set his mind at rest upon that. Moreover, don't fool yourself that I'm going to stay around here. Inside of six hours I'll be over those mountains, if I have to gnaw a passage through them, and on my way East.'

They had both got to their feet, and at this remark Kismine came close and put her arm through his.

'I'm going, too.'

'You must be crazy——'

'Of course I'm going,' she interrupted patiently.

'You most certainly are not. You——'

'Very well,' she said quietly, 'we'll catch up with father now and talk it over with him.'

Defeated, John mustered a sickly smile.

'Very well, dearest,' he agreed, with pale and unconvincing affection, 'we'll go together.'

His love for her returned and settled placidly on his heart. She was his—she would go with him to share his dangers. He put his arms about her and kissed her fervently. After all she loved him; she had saved him, in fact.

Discussing the matter, they walked slowly back towards the château. They decided that since Braddock Washington had seen them together they had best depart the next night. Nevertheless, John's lips were unusually dry at dinner, and he nervously emptied a great spoonful of peacock soup into his left lung. He had to be carried into the turquoise and sable card-room and pounded on the back by one of the under-butlers, which Percy considered a great joke.

IX

Long after midnight John's body gave a nervous jerk, and he sat suddenly upright, staring into the veils of somnolence that draped the room. Through the squares of blue darkness that were his open windows, he had heard a faint faraway sound that died upon a bed of wind before identifying itself on his memory, clouded with uneasy dreams. But the sharp noise that had succeeded it was nearer, was just outside the room—the click of a turned knob, a footstep, a whisper, he could not tell; a hard lump gathered in the pit of his stomach, and his whole body ached in the moment that he strained agonizingly to hear. Then one of the veils seemed to dissolve, and he saw a vague figure standing by the door, a figure only faintly limned and blocked in upon the darkness, mingled so with the folds of the drapery as to seem distorted, like a reflection seen in a dirty pane of glass.

With a sudden movement of fright or resolution John

pressed the button by his bedside, and the next moment he
was sitting in the green sunken bath of the adjoining room,
waked into alertness by the shock of the cold water which
half filled it.

He sprang out, and, his wet pyjamas scattering a heavy
trickle of water behind him, ran for the aquamarine door
which he knew led out onto the ivory landing of the second
floor. The door opened noiselessly. A single crimson lamp
burning in a great dome above it lit the magnificent sweep of
the carved stairways with a poignant beauty. For a moment
John hesitated, appalled by the silent splendour massed
about him, seeming to envelop in its gigantic folds and
contours the solitary drenched little figure shivering upon
the ivory landing. Then simultaneously two things happened. The door of his own sitting-room swung open,
precipitating three naked negroes into the hall—and, as John
swayed in wild terror towards the stairway, another door
slid back in the wall on the other side of the corridor, and
John saw Braddock Washington standing in the lighted lift,
wearing a fur coat and a pair of riding boots which reached
to his knees and displayed, above, the glow of his rose-
coloured pyjamas.

On the instant the three negroes—John had never seen
any of them before, and it flashed through his mind that
they must be the professional executioners—paused in their
movement towards John, and turned expectantly to the man
in the lift, who burst out with an imperious command :

'Get in here! All three of you! Quick as hell!'

Then, within the instant, the three negroes darted into
the cage, the oblong of light was blotted out as the lift door
slid shut, and John was again alone in the hall. He slumped
weakly down against an ivory stair.

It was apparent that something portentous had occurred,
something which, for the moment at least, had postponed
his own petty disaster. What was it? Had the negroes risen
in revolt? Had the aviators forced aside the iron bars of the
grating? Or had the men of Fish stumbled blindly through
the hills and gazed with bleak, joyless eyes upon the gaudy

valley? John did not know. He heard a faint whir of air as the lift whizzed up again, and then, a moment later, as it descended. It was probable that Percy was hurrying to his father's assistance, and it occurred to John that this was his opportunity to join Kismine and plan an immediate escape. He waited until the lift had been silent for several minutes; shivering a little with the night cool that whipped in through his wet pyjamas, he returned to his room and dressed himself quickly. Then he mounted a long flight of stairs and turned down the corridor carpeted with Russian sable which led to Kismine's suite.

The door of her sitting-room was open and the lamps were lighted. Kismine, in an angora kimono, stood near the window of the room in a listening attitude, and as John entered noiselessly, she turned towards him.

'Oh, it's you!' she whispered, crossing the room to him. 'Did you hear them?'

'I heard your father's slaves in my——'

'No,' she interrupted excitedly. 'Aeroplanes!'

'Aeroplanes? Perhaps that was the sound that woke me.'

'There're at least a dozen. I saw one a few moments ago dead against the moon. The guard back by the cliff fired his rifle and that's what roused father. We're going to open on them right away.'

'Are they here on purpose?'

'Yes—it's that Italian who got away——'

Simultaneously with her last word, a succession of sharp cracks tumbled in through the open window. Kismine uttered a little cry, took a penny with fumbling fingers from a box on her dresser, and ran to one of the electric lights. In an instant the entire château was in darkness—she had blown out the fuse.

'Come on!' she cried to him. 'We'll go up to the roof garden, and watch it from there!'

Drawing a cape about her, she took his hand, and they found their way out the door. It was only a step to the tower lift, and as she pressed the button that shot them upward he put his arms around her in the darkness and kissed her

3*

mouth. Romance had come to John Unger at last. A minute later they had stepped out upon the star-white platform. Above, under the misty moon, sliding in and out of the patches of cloud that eddied below it, floated a dozen dark-winged bodies in a constant circling course. From here and there in the valley flashes of fire leaped towards them, followed by sharp detonations. Kismine clapped her hands with pleasure, which a moment later, turned to dismay as the aeroplanes at some prearranged signal, began to release their bombs and the whole of the valley became a panorama of deep reverberant sound and lurid light.

Before long the aim of the attackers became concentrated upon the points where the anti-aircraft guns were situated, and one of them was almost immediately reduced to a giant cinder to lie smouldering in a park of rose bushes.

'Kismine,' begged John, 'you'll be glad when I tell you that this attack came on the eve of my murder. If I hadn't heard that guard shoot off his gun back by the pass I should now be stone dead——'

'I can't hear you!' cried Kismine, intent on the scene before her. 'You'll have to talk louder!'

'I simply said,' shouted John, 'that we'd better get out before they begin to shell the Château!'

Suddenly the whole portico of the negro quarters cracked asunder, a geyser of flame shot up from under the colonnades, and great fragments of jagged marble were hurled as far as the borders of the lake.

'There go fifty thousand dollars' worth of slaves,' cried Kismine, 'at pre-war prices. So few Americans have any respect for property.'

John renewed his efforts to compel her to leave. The aim of the aeroplanes was becoming more precise minute by minute, and only two of the anti-aircraft guns were still retaliating. It was obvious that the garrison, encircled with fire, could not hold out much longer.

'Come on!' cried John, pulling Kismine's arm, 'we've got to go. Do you realize that those aviators will kill you without question if they find you?'

She consented reluctantly.

'We'll have to wake Jasmine!' she said, as they hurried towards the lift. Then she added in a sort of childish delight: 'We'll be poor, won't we? Like people in books. And I'll be an orphan and utterly free. Free and poor! What fun!' She stopped and raised her lips to him in a delighted kiss.

'It's impossible to be both together,' said John grimly. 'People have found that out. And I should choose to be free as preferable of the two. As an extra caution you'd better dump the contents of your jewel box into your pockets.'

Ten minutes later the two girls met John in the dark corridor and they descended to the main floor of the château. Passing for the last time through the magnificence of the splendid halls, they stood for a moment out on the terrace, watching the burning negro quarters and the flaming embers of two planes which had fallen on the other side of the lake. A solitary gun was still keeping up a sturdy popping, and the attackers seemed timorous about descending lower, but sent their thunderous fireworks in a circle around it, until any chance shot might annihilate its Ethiopian crew.

John and the two sisters passed down the marble steps, turned sharply to the left, and began to ascend a narrow path that wound like a garter about the diamond mountain. Kismine knew a heavily wooded spot half-way up where they could lie concealed and yet be able to observe the wild night in the valley—finally to make an escape, when it should be necessary, along a secret path laid in a rocky gully.

X

It was three o'clock when they attained their destination. The obliging and phlegmatic Jasmine fell off to sleep immediately, leaning against the trunk of a large tree, while John and Kismine sat, his arm around her, and watched the desperate ebb and flow of the dying battle among the ruins of a vista that had been a garden spot that morning. Shortly

after four o'clock the last remaining gun gave out a clanging
sound and went out of action in a swift tongue of red smoke.
Though the moon was down, they saw that the flying bodies
were circling closer to the earth. When the planes had made
certain that the beleaguered possessed no further resources,
they would land and the dark and glittering reign of the
Washingtons would be over.

With the cessation of the firing the valley grew quiet.
The embers of the two aeroplanes glowed like the eyes of
some monster crouching in the grass. The château stood
dark and silent, beautiful without light as it had been
beautiful in the sun, while the woody rattles of Nemesis
filled the air above with a growing and receding complaint.
Then John perceived that Kismine, like her sister, had
fallen sound asleep.

It was long after four when he became aware of footsteps
along the path they had lately followed, and he waited in
breathless silence until the persons to whom they belonged
had passed the vantage-point he occupied. There was a faint
stir in the air now that was not of human origin, and the
dew was cold; he knew that the dawn would break soon.
John waited until the steps had gone a safe distance up the
mountain and were inaudible. Then he followed. About
half-way to the steep summit the trees fell away and a hard
saddle of rock spread itself over the diamond beneath. Just
before he reached this point he slowed down his pace,
warned by an animal sense that there was life just ahead
of him. Coming to a high boulder, he lifted his head
gradually above its edge. His curiosity was rewarded; this
is what he saw:

Braddock Washington was standing there motionless,
silhouetted against the grey sky without sound or sign of
life. As the dawn came up out of the east, lending a cold
green colour to the earth, it brought the solitary figure into
insignificant contrast with the new day.

While John watched, his host remained for a few moments
absorbed in some inscrutable contemplation; then he signalled to the two negroes who crouched at his feet to lift

the burden which lay between them. As they struggled upright, the first yellow beam of the sun struck through the innumerable prisms of an immense and exquisitely chiselled diamond—and a white radiance was kindled that glowed upon the air like a fragment of the morning star. The bearers staggered beneath its weight for a moment—then their rippling muscles caught and hardened under the wet shine of the skins and the three figures were again motionless in their defiant impotency before the heavens.

After a while the white man lifted his head and slowly raised his arms in a gesture of attention, as one who would call a great crowd to hear—but there was no crowd, only the vast silence of the mountain and the sky, broken by faint bird voices down among the trees. The figure on the saddle of rock began to speak ponderously and with an inextinguishable pride.

'You out there—' he cried in a trembling voice. 'You—there—!' He paused, his arms still uplifted, his head held attentively as though he were expecting an answer. John strained his eyes to see whether there might be men coming down the mountain, but the mountain was bare of human life. There was only sky and a mocking flute of wind along the tree-tops. Could Washington be praying? For a moment John wondered. Then the illusion passed—there was something in the man's whole attitude antithetical to prayer.

'Oh, you above there!'

The voice was become strong and confident. This was no forlorn supplication. If anything, there was in it a quality of monstrous condescension.

'You there——'

Words, too quickly uttered to be understood, flowing one into the other. . . . John listened breathlessly, catching a phrase here and there, while the voice broke off, resumed, broke off again—now strong and argumentative, now coloured with a slow, puzzled impatience. Then a conviction commenced to dawn on the single listener, and as realization crept over him a spray of quick blood rushed through his arteries. Braddock Washington was offering a bribe to God!

That was it—there was no doubt. The diamond in the arms of his slaves was some advance sample, a promise of more to follow.

That, John perceived after a time, was the thread running through his sentences. Prometheus Enriched was calling to witness forgotten sacrifices, forgotten rituals, prayers obsolete before the birth of Christ. For a while his discourse took the form of reminding God of this gift or that which Divinity had deigned to accept from men—great churches if he would rescue cities from the plague, gifts of myrrh and gold, of human lives and beautiful women and captive armies, of children and queens, of beasts of the forest and field, sheep and goats, harvests and cities, whole conquered lands that had been offered up in lust or blood for His appeasal, buying a meed's worth of alleviation from the Divine wrath—and now he, Braddock Washington, Emperor of Diamonds, king and priest of the age of gold, arbiter of splendour and luxury, would offer up a treasure such as princes before him had never dreamed of, offer it up not in suppliance, but in pride.

He would give to God, he continued, getting down to specifications, the greatest diamond in the world. This diamond would be cut with many more thousand facets than there were leaves on a tree, and yet the whole diamond would be shaped with the perfection of a stone no bigger than a fly. Many men would work upon it for many years. It would be set in a great dome of beaten gold, wonderfully carved and equipped with gates of opal and crusted sapphire. In the middle would be hollowed out a chapel presided over by an altar of iridescent, decomposing, ever-changing radium which would burn out the eyes of any worshipper who lifted up his head from prayer—and on this altar there would be slain for the amusement of the Divine Benefactor any victim He should choose, even though it should be the greatest and most powerful man alive.

In return he asked only a simple thing, a thing that for God would be absurdly easy—only that matters should be as they were yesterday at this hour and that they should so remain. So very simple! Let but the heavens open, swallowing these men and their aeroplanes—and then close again. Let him have his slaves once more, restored to life and well.

There was no one else with whom he had ever needed to treat or bargain.

He doubted only whether he had made his bribe big enough. God had His price, of course. God was made in man's image, so it had been said: He must have His price. And the price would be rare—no cathedral whose building consumed many years, no pyramid constructed by ten thousand workmen, would be like this cathedral, this pyramid.

He paused here. That was his proposition. Everything would be up to specifications and there was nothing vulgar in his assertion that it would be cheap at the price. He implied that Providence could take it or leave it.

As he approached the end his sentences became broken, became short and uncertain, and his body seemed tense, seemed strained to catch the slightest pressure or whisper of life in the spaces around him. His hair had turned gradually white as he talked, and now he lifted his head high to the heavens like a prophet of old—magnificently mad.

Then, as John stared in giddy fascination, it seemed to him that a curious phenomenon took place somewhere around him. It was as though the sky had darkened for an instant, as though there had been a sudden murmur in a gust of wind, a sound of far-away trumpets, a sighing like the rustle of a great silken robe—for a time the whole of nature round about partook of this darkness: the birds' song ceased; the trees were still, and far over the mountain there was a mutter of dull, menacing thunder.

That was all. The wind died along the tall grasses of the valley. The dawn and the day resumed their place in a time, and the risen sun sent hot waves of yellow mist that made its path bright before it. The leaves laughed in the sun, and their laughter shook the trees until each bough was like a girls' school in fairyland. God had refused to accept the bribe.

For another moment John watched the triumph of the

day. Then, turning, he saw a flutter of brown down by the lake, then another flutter, then another, like the dance of golden angels alighting from the clouds. The aeroplanes had come to earth.

John slid off the boulder and ran down the side of the mountain to the clump of trees, where the two girls were awake and waiting for him. Kismine sprang to her feet, the jewels in her pockets jingling, a question on her parted lips, but instinct told John that there was no time for words. They must get off the mountain without losing a moment. He seized a hand of each, and in silence they threaded the tree-trunks, washed with light now and with the rising mist. Behind them from the valley came no sound at all, except the complaint of the peacocks far away and the pleasant undertone of morning.

When they had gone about a half a mile, they avoided the park land and entered a narrow path that led over the next rise of ground. At the highest point of this they paused and turned around. Their eyes rested upon the mountainside they had just left—oppressed by some dark sense of tragic impendency.

Clear against the sky a broken, white-haired man was slowly descending the steep slope, followed by two gigantic and emotionless negroes, who carried a burden between them which still flashed and glittered in the sun. Half-way down two other figures joined them—John could see that they were Mrs Washington and her son, upon whose arm she leaned. The aviators had clambered from their machines to the sweeping lawn in front of the château, and with rifles in hand were starting up the diamond mountain in skirmishing formation.

But the little group of five which had formed farther up and was engrossing all the watchers' attention had stopped upon a ledge of rock. The negroes stooped and pulled up what appeared to be a trapdoor in the side of the mountain. Into this they all disappeared, the white-haired man first, then his wife and son, finally the two negroes, the glittering tips of whose jewelled head-dresses caught the sun for a moment before the trap-door descended and engulfed them all.

Kismine clutched John's arm.

'Oh,' she cried wildly, 'where are they going? What are they going to do?'

'It must be some underground way of escape——'

A little scream from the two girls interrupted his sentence.

'Don't you see?' sobbed Kismine hysterically. 'The mountain is wired!'

Even as she spoke John put up his hands to shield his sight. Before their eyes the whole surface of the mountain had changed suddenly to a dazzling burning yellow, which showed up through the jacket of turf as light shows through a human hand. For a moment the intolerable glow continued, and then like an extinguished filament it disappeared, revealing a black waste from which blue smoke arose slowly, carrying off with it what remained of vegetation and of human flesh. Of the aviators there was left neither blood nor bone—they were consumed as completely as the five souls who had gone inside.

Simultaneously, and with an immense concussion, the château literally threw itself into the air, bursting into flaming fragments as it rose, and then tumbling back upon itself in a smoking pile that lay projecting half into the water of the lake. There was no fire—what smoke there was drifted off mingling with the sunshine, and for a few minutes longer a powdery dust of marble drifted from the great featureless pile that had once been the house of jewels. There was no more sound and the three people were alone in the valley.

XI

At sunset John and his two companions reached the high cliff which had marked the boundaries of the Washingtons' dominion, and looking back found the valley tranquil and lovely in the dusk. They sat down to finish the food which Jasmine had brought with her in a basket.

'There!' she said, as she spread the tablecloth and put

the sandwiches in a neat pile upon it. 'Don't they look tempting? I always think that food tastes better outdoors.'

'With that remark,' remarked Kismine, 'Jasmine enters the middle class.'

'Now,' said John eagerly, 'turn out your pockets and let's see what jewels you brought along. If you made a good selection we three ought to live comfortably all the rest of our lives.'

Obediently Kismine put her hand in her pocket and tossed two handfuls of glittering stones before him.

'Not so bad,' cried John, enthusiastically. 'They aren't very big, but—Hello!' His expression changed as he held one of them up to the declining sun. 'Why, these aren't diamonds! There's something the matter!'

'By golly!' exclaimed Kismine, with a startled look. 'What an idiot I am!'

'Why, these are rhinestones!' cried John.

'I know.' She broke into a laugh. 'I opened the wrong drawer. They belonged on the dress of a girl who visited Jasmine. I got her to give them to me in exchange for diamonds. I'd never seen anything but precious stones before.'

'And this is what you brought?'

'I'm afraid so.' She fingered the brilliants wistfully. 'I think I like these better. I'm a little tired of diamonds.'

'Very well,' said John gloomily. 'We'll have to live in Hades. And you will grow old telling incredulous women that you got the wrong drawer. Unfortunately your father's bank-books were consumed with him.'

'Well, what's the matter with Hades?'

'If I come home with a wife at my age my father is just as liable as not to cut me off with a hot coal, as they say down there.'

Jasmine spoke up.

'I love washing,' she said quietly. 'I have always washed my own handkerchiefs. I'll take in laundry and support you both.'

'Do they have washwomen in Hades?' asked Kismine innocently.

'Of course,' answered John. 'It's just like anywhere else.'

'I thought—perhaps it was too hot to wear any clothes.' John laughed.

'Just try it!' he suggested. 'They'll run you out before you're half started.'

'Will father be there?' she asked.

John turned to her in astonishment.

'Your father is dead,' he replied sombrely. 'Why should he go to Hades? You have it confused with another place that was abolished long ago.'

After supper they folded up the table-cloth and spread their blankets for the night.

'What a dream it was,' Kismine sighed, gazing up at the stars. 'How strange it seems to be here with one dress and a penniless fiancé!

'Under the stars,' she repeated. 'I never noticed the stars before. I always thought of them as great big diamonds that belonged to someone. Now they frighten me. They make me feel that it was all a dream, all my youth.'

'It *was* a dream,' said John quietly. 'Everybody's youth is a dream, a form of chemical madness.'

'How pleasant then to be insane!'

'So I'm told,' said John gloomily. 'I don't know any longer. At any rate, let us love for a while, for a year or so, you and me. That's a form of divine drunkenness that we can all try. There are only diamonds in the whole world, diamonds and perhaps the shabby gift of disillusion. Well, I have that last and I will make the usual nothing of it.' He shivered. 'Turn up your coat collar, little girl, the night's full of chill and you'll get pneumonia. His was a great sin who first invented consciousness. Let us lose it for a few hours.'

So wrapping himself in his blanket he fell off to sleep.

BERNICE BOBS HER HAIR

[1920]

AFTER dark on Saturday night one could stand on the first tee of the golf-course and see the country-club windows as a yellow expanse over a very black and wavy ocean. The waves of this ocean, so to speak, were the heads of many curious caddies, a few of the more ingenious chauffeurs, the golf professional's deaf sister— and there were usually several stray, diffident waves who might have rolled inside had they so desired. This was the gallery.

The balcony was inside. It consisted of the circle of wicker chairs that lined the wall of the combination clubroom and ballroom. At these Saturday-night dances it was largely feminine; a great babel of middle-aged ladies with sharp eyes and icy hearts behind lorgnettes and large bosoms. The main function of the balcony was critical. It occasionally showed grudging admiration, but never approval, for it is well known among ladies over thirty-five that when the younger set dance in the summer-time it is with the very worst intentions in the world, and if they are not bombarded with stony eyes stray couples will dance weird barbaric interludes in the corners, and the more popular, more dangerous, girls will sometimes be kissed in the parked limousines of unsuspecting dowagers.

But, after all, this critical circle is not close enough to the stage to see the actors' faces and catch the subtler byplay. It can only frown and lean, ask questions and make satisfactory deductions from its set of postulates, such as the one which states that every young man with a large income leads the life of a hunted partridge. It never really appreciates the drama of the shifting, semi-cruel world of adolescence. No; boxes, orchestra-circle, principals, and chorus are represented by the medley of faces and voices that sway to the plaintive African rhythm of Dyer's dance orchestra.

From sixteen-year-old Otis Ormonde, who has two more years at Hill School, to G. Reece Stoddard, over whose bureau at home hangs a Harvard law diploma; from little Madeleine Hogue, whose hair still feels strange and uncomfortable on top of her head, to Bessie MacRae, who has been the life of the party a little too long—more than ten years—the medley is not only the centre of the stage but contains the only people capable of getting an unobstructed view of it.

With a flourish and a bang the music stops. The couples exchange artificial, effortless smiles, facetiously repeat '*la-de-da-da* dum-*dum*,' and then the clatter of young feminine voices soars over the burst of clapping.

A few disappointed stags caught in midfloor as they had been about to cut in subsided listlessly back to the walls, because this was not like the riotous Christmas dances—these summer hops were considered just pleasantly warm and exciting, where even the younger marrieds rose and performed ancient waltzes and terrifying fox trots to the tolerant amusement of their younger brothers and sisters.

Warren McIntyre, who casually attended Yale, being one of the unfortunate stags, felt in his dinner-coat pocket for a cigarette and strolled out onto the wide, semidark veranda, where couples were scattered at tables, filling the lantern-hung night with vague words and hazy laughter. He nodded here and there at the less absorbed and as he passed each couple some half-forgotten fragment of a story played in his mind, for it was not a large city and every one was Who's Who to every one else's past. There, for example, were Jim Strain and Ethel Demorest, who had been privately engaged for three years. Every one knew that as soon as Jim managed to

hold a job for more than two months she would marry
him. Yet how bored they both looked, and how wearily
Ethel regarded Jim sometimes, as if she wondered why
she had trained the vines of her affection on such a wind-
shaken poplar.

Warren was nineteen and rather pitying with those of
his friends who hadn't gone East to college. But, like
most boys, he bragged tremendously about the girls of
his city when he was away from it. There was Genevieve
Ormonde, who regularly made the rounds of dances,
house-parties, and football games at Princeton, Yale, Wil-
liams, and Cornell; there was black-eyed Roberta Dillon,
who was quite as famous to her own generation as Hiram
Johnson or Ty Cobb; and, of course, there was Marjorie
Harvey, who besides having a fairylike face and a dazzling,
bewildering tongue was already justly celebrated for
having turned five cart-wheels in succession during the
past pump-and-slipper dance at New Haven.

Warren, who had grown up across the street from
Marjorie, had long been 'crazy about her.' Sometimes she
seemed to reciprocate his feeling with a faint gratitude,
but she had tried him by her infallible test and informed
him gravely that she did not love him. Her test was that
when she was away from him she forgot him and had
affairs with other boys. Warren found this discouraging,
especially as Marjorie had been making little trips all
summer, and for the first two or three days after each
arrival home he saw great heaps of mail on the Harveys'
hall table addressed to her in various masculine hand-
writings. To make matters worse, all during the month
of August she had been visited by her cousin Bernice
from Eau Claire, and it seemed impossible to see her
alone. It was always necessary to hunt round and find
some one to take care of Bernice. As August waned this
was becoming more and more difficult.

Much as Warren worshipped Marjorie, he had to admit
that Cousin Bernice was sorta dopeless. She was pretty,
with dark hair and high colour, but she was no fun on a

party. Every Saturday night he danced a long arduous
duty dance with her to please Marjorie, but he had never
been anything but bored in her company.

'Warren'—a soft voice at his elbow broke in upon his
thoughts, and he turned to see Marjorie, flushed and
radiant as usual. She laid a hand on his shoulder and a
glow settled almost imperceptibly over him.

'Warren,' she whispered, 'do something for me—dance
with Bernice. She's been stuck with little Otis Ormonde
for almost an hour.'

Warren's glow faded.

'Why—sure,' he answered half-heartedly.

'You don't mind, do you? I'll see that you don't get
stuck.'

' 'Sall right.'

Marjorie smiled—that smile that was thanks enough.

'You're an angel, and I'm obliged loads.'

With a sigh the angel glanced round the veranda, but
Bernice and Otis were not in sight. He wandered back
inside, and there in front of the women's dressing-
room he found Otis in the centre of a group of young
men who were convulsed with laughter. Otis was brandish-
ing a piece of timber he had picked up, and discoursing
volubly.

'She's gone in to fix her hair,' he announced wildly.
'I'm waiting to dance another hour with her.'

Their laughter was renewed.

'Why don't some of you cut in?' cried Otis resentfully.
'She likes more variety.'

'Why, Otis,' suggested a friend, 'you've just barely got
used to her.'

'Why the two-by-four, Otis?' inquired Warren, smiling.

'The two-by-four? Oh, this? This is a club. When she
comes out I'll hit her on the head and knock her in
again.'

Warren collapsed on a settee and howled with glee.

'Never mind, Otis,' he articulated finally. 'I'm relieving
you this time.'

Otis simulated a sudden fainting attack and handed the stick to Warren.

'If you need it, old man,' he said hoarsely.

No matter how beautiful or brilliant a girl may be, the reputation of not being frequently cut in on makes her position at a dance unfortunate. Perhaps boys prefer her company to that of the butterflies with whom they dance a dozen times an evening, but youth in this jazz-nourished generation is temperamentally restless, and the idea of fox-trotting more than one full fox trot with the same girl is distasteful, not to say odious. When it comes to several dances and the intermissions between she can be quite sure that a young man, once relieved, will never tread on her wayward toes again.

Warren danced the next full dance with Bernice, and finally, thankful for the intermission, he led her to a table on the veranda. There was a moment's silence while she did unimpressive things with her fan.

'It's hotter here than in Eau Claire,' she said.

Warren stifled a sigh and nodded. It might be for all he knew or cared. He wondered idly whether she was a poor conversationalist because she got no attention or got no attention because she was a poor conversationalist.

'You going to be here much longer?' he asked, and then turned rather red. She might suspect his reasons for asking.

'Another week,' she answered, and stared at him as if to lunge at his next remark when it left his lips.

Warren fidgeted. Then with a sudden charitable impulse he decided to try part of his line on her. He turned and looked at her eyes.

'You've got an awfully kissable mouth,' he began quietly.

This was a remark that he sometimes made to girls at college proms when they were talking in just such half dark as this. Bernice distinctly jumped. She turned an ungraceful red and became clumsy with her fan. No one had ever made such a remark to her before.

'Fresh!'—the word had slipped out before she realized

it, and she bit her lip. Too late she decided to be amused, and offered him a flustered smile.

Warren was annoyed. Though not accustomed to have that remark taken seriously, still it usually provoked a laugh or a paragraph of sentimental banter. And he hated to be called fresh, except in a joking way. His charitable impulse died and he switched the topic.

'Jim Strain and Ethel Demorest sitting out as usual,' he commented.

This was more in Bernice's line, but a faint regret mingled with her relief as the subject changed. Men did not talk to her about kissable mouths, but she knew that they talked in some such way to other girls.

'Oh, yes,' she said, and laughed. 'I hear they've been mooning round for years without a red penny. Isn't it silly?'

Warren's disgust increased. Jim Strain was a close friend of his brother's, and anyway he considered it bad form to sneer at people for not having money. But Bernice had had no intention of sneering. She was merely nervous.

II

When Marjorie and Bernice reached home at half after midnight they said good night at the top of the stairs. Though cousins, they were not intimates. As a matter of fact Marjorie had no female intimates—she considered girls stupid. Bernice on the contrary all through this parent-arranged visit had rather longed to exchange those confidences flavoured with giggles and tears that she considered an indispensable factor in all feminine intercourse. But in this respect she found Marjorie rather cold; felt somehow the same difficulty in talking to her that she had in talking to men Marjorie never giggled, was never frightened, seldom embarrassed, and in fact had very few of the qualities which Bernice considered appropriately and blessedly feminine.

As Bernice busied herself with tooth-brush and paste

this night she wondered for the hundredth time why she never had any attention when she was away from home. That her family were the wealthiest in Eau Claire; that her mother entertained tremendously, gave little dinners for her daughter before all dances and bought her a car of her own to drive round in, never occurred to her as factors in her home-town social success. Like most girls she had been brought up on the warm milk prepared by Annie Fellows Johnston and on novels in which the female was beloved because of certain mysterious womanly qualities, always mentioned but never displayed.

Bernice felt a vague pain that she was not at present engaged in being popular. She did not know that had it not been for Marjorie's campaigning she would have danced the entire evening with one man; but she knew that even in Eau Claire other girls with less position and less pulchritude were given a much bigger rush. She attributed this to something subtly unscrupulous in those girls. It had never worried her, and if it had her mother would have assured her that the other girls cheapened themselves and that men really respected girls like Bernice.

She turned out the light in her bathroom, and on an impulse decided to go in and chat for a moment with her aunt Josephine, whose light was still on. Her soft slippers bore her noiselessly down the carpeted hall, but hearing voices inside she stopped near the partly opened door. Then she caught her own name, and without any definite intention of eavesdropping lingered—and the thread of the conversation going on inside pierced her consciousness sharply as if it had been drawn through with a needle.

'She's absolutely hopeless!' It was Marjorie's voice. 'Oh, I know what you're going to say! So many people have told you how pretty and sweet she is, and how she can cook! What of it? She has a bum time. Men don't like her.'

'What's a little cheap popularity?'

Mrs Harvey sounded annoyed.

'It's everything when you're eighteen,' said Marjorie emphatically. 'I've done my best. I've been polite and I've made men dance with her, but they just won't stand being bored. When I think of that gorgeous colouring wasted on such a ninny, and think what Martha Carey could do with it—oh!'

'There's no courtesy these days.'

Mrs Harvey's voice implied that modern situations were too much for her. When she was a girl all young ladies who belonged to nice families had glorious times.

'Well,' said Marjorie, 'no girl can permanently bolster up a lame-duck visitor, because these days it's every girl for herself. I've even tried to drop her hints about clothes and things, and she's been furious—given me the funniest looks. She's sensitive enough to know she's not getting away with much, but I'll bet she consoles herself by thinking that she's very virtuous and that I'm too gay and fickle and will come to a bad end. All unpopular girls think that way. Sour grapes! Sarah Hopkins refers to Genevieve and Roberta and me as gardenia girls! I'll bet she'd give ten years of her life and her European education to be a gardenia girl and have three or four men in love with her and be cut in on every few feet at dances.'

'It seems to me,' interrupted Mrs Harvey rather wearily, 'that you ought to be able to do something for Bernice. I know she's not very vivacious.'

Marjorie groaned.

'Vivacious! Good grief! I've never heard her say anything to a boy except that it's hot or the floor's crowded or that she's going to school in New York next year. Sometimes she asks them what kind of car they have and tells them the kind she has. Thrilling!'

There was a short silence, and then Mrs Harvey took up her refrain:

'All I know is that other girls not half so sweet and attractive get partners. Martha Carey, for instance, is stout and loud, and her mother is distinctly common. Roberta Dillon is so thin this year that she looks as though Arizona were the place for her. She's dancing herself to death.'

'But, mother,' objected Marjorie impatiently, 'Martha is cheerful and awfully witty and an awfully slick girl, and Roberta's a marvellous dancer. She's been popular for ages!'

Mrs Harvey yawned.

'I think it's that crazy Indian blood in Bernice,' continued Marjorie. 'Maybe she's a reversion to type. Indian women all just sat round and never said anything.'

'Go to bed, you silly child,' laughed Mrs Harvey. 'I wouldn't have told you that if I'd thought you were going to remember it. And I think most of your ideas are perfectly idiotic,' she finished sleepily.

There was another silence, while Marjorie considered whether or not convincing her mother was worth the trouble. People over forty can seldom be permanently convinced of anything. At eighteen our convictions are hills from which we look; at forty-five they are caves in which we hide.

Having decided this, Marjorie said good night. When she came out into the hall it was quite empty.

III

While Marjorie was breakfasting late next day Bernice came into the room with a rather formal good morning, sat down opposite, stared intently over and slightly moistened her lips.

'What's on your mind?' inquired Marjorie, rather puzzled.

Bernice paused before she threw her hand-grenade.

'I heard what you said about me to your mother last night.'

Marjorie was startled, but she showed only a faintly heightened colour and her voice was quite even when she spoke.

'Where were you?'

'In the hall. I didn't mean to listen—at first.'

After an involuntary look of contempt Marjorie dropped her eyes and became very interested in balancing a stray corn-flake on her finger.

'I guess I'd better go back to Eau Claire—if I'm such a nuisance.' Bernice's lower lip was trembling violently and she continued on a wavering note: 'I've tried to be nice, and—and I've been first neglected and then insulted. No one ever visited me and got such treatment.'

Marjorie was silent.

'But I'm in the way, I see. I'm a drag on you. Your friends don't like me.' She paused, and then remembered another one of her grievances. 'Of course I was furious last week when you tried to hint to me that that dress was unbecoming. Don't you think I know how to dress myself?'

'No,' murmured Marjorie less than half-aloud.

'What?'

'I didn't hint anything,' said Marjorie succinctly. 'I said, as I remember, that it was better to wear a becoming dress three times straight than to alternate it with two frights.'

'Do you think that was a very nice thing to say?'

'I wasn't trying to be nice.' Then after a pause: 'When do you want to go?'

Bernice drew in her breath sharply.

'Oh!' It was a little half-cry.

Marjorie looked up in surprise.

'Didn't you say you were going?'

'Yes, but——'

'Oh, you were only bluffing!'

They stared at each other across the breakfast-table for a moment. Misty waves were passing before Bernice's eyes, while Marjorie's face wore that rather hard expression that she used when slightly intoxicated undergraduates were making love to her.

'So you were bluffing,' she repeated as if it were what she might have expected.

Bernice admitted it by bursting into tears. Marjorie's eyes showed boredom.

'You're my cousin,' sobbed Bernice. 'I'm v-v-visiting you. I was to stay a month, and if I go home my mother will know and she'll wah-wonder——'

Marjorie waited until the shower of broken words collapsed into little sniffles.

'I'll give you my month's allowance,' she said coldly, 'and you can spend this last week anywhere you want. There's a very nice hotel——'

Bernice's sobs rose to a flute note, and rising of a sudden she fled from the room.

An hour later, while Marjorie was in the library absorbed in composing one of those non-committal, marvellously elusive letters that only a young girl can write, Bernice reappeared, very red-eyed and consciously calm. She cast no glance at Marjorie but took a book at random from the shelf and sat down as if to read. Marjorie seemed absorbed in her letter and continued writing. When the clock showed noon Bernice closed her book with a snap.

'I suppose I'd better get my railroad ticket.'

This was not the beginning of the speech she had rehearsed upstairs, but as Marjorie was not getting her cues—wasn't urging her to be reasonable; it's all a mistake —it was the best opening she could muster.

'Just wait till I finish this letter,' said Marjorie without looking round. 'I want to get it off in the next mail.'

After another minute, during which her pen scratched busily, she turned round and relaxed with an air of 'at your service.' Again Bernice had to speak.

'Do you want me to go home?'

'Well,' said Marjorie, considering, 'I suppose if you're not having a good time you'd better go. No use being miserable.'

'Don't you think common kindness——'

'Oh, please don't quote "Little Women"!' cried Marjorie impatiently. 'That's out of style.'

'You think so?'

'Heavens, yes! What modern girl could live like those inane females?'

'They were the models for our mothers.'

Marjorie laughed.

'Yes, they were—not! Besides, our mothers were all very well in their way, but they know very little about their daughters' problems.'

Bernice drew herself up.

'Please don't talk about my mother.'

Marjorie laughed.

'I don't think I mentioned her.'

Bernice felt that she was being led away from her subject.

'Do you think you've treated me very well?'

'I've done my best. You're rather hard material to work with.'

The lids of Bernice's eyes reddened.

'I think you're hard and selfish, and you haven't a feminine quality in you.'

'Oh, my Lord!' cried Marjorie in desperation. 'You little nut! Girls like you are responsible for all the tiresome colourless marriages; all those ghastly inefficiencies that pass as feminine qualities. What a blow it must be when a man with imagination marries the beautiful bundle of clothes that he's been building ideals round, and finds that she's just a weak, whining, cowardly mass of affectations!'

Bernice's mouth had slipped half open.

'The womanly woman!' continued Marjorie. 'Her whole early life is occupied in whining criticisms of girls like me who really do have a good time.'

Bernice's jaw descended farther as Marjorie's voice rose.

'There's some excuse for an ugly girl whining. If I'd been irretrievably ugly I'd never have forgiven my parents for bringing me into the world. But you're starting life without any handicap—' Marjorie's little fist clinched. 'If you expect me to weep with you you'll be disappointed.

Go or stay, just as you like.' And picking up her letters she left the room.

Bernice claimed a headache and failed to apppear at luncheon. They had a matinée date for the afternoon, but the headache persisting, Marjorie made explanations to a not very downcast boy. But when she returned late in the afternoon she found Bernice with a strangely set face waiting for her in her bedroom.

'I've decided,' began Bernice without preliminaries, 'that maybe you're right about things—possibly not. But if you'll tell me why your friends aren't—aren't interested in me I'll see if I can do what you want me to.'

Marjorie was at the mirror shaking down her hair.

'Do you mean it?'

'Yes.'

'Without reservations? Will you do exactly what I say?'

'Well, I——'

'Well nothing! Will you do exactly as I say?'

'If they're sensible things.'

'They're not! You're no case for sensible things.'

'Are you going to make—to recommend——'

'Yes, everything. If I tell you to take boxing lessons you'll have to do it. Write home and tell your mother you're going to stay another two weeks.'

'If you'll tell me——'

'All right—I'll just give you a few examples now. First, you have no ease of manner. Why? Because you're never sure about your personal appearance. When a girl feels that she's perfectly groomed and dressed she can forget that part of her. That's charm. The more parts of yourself you can afford to forget the more charm you have.'

'Don't I look all right?'

'No; for instance, you never take care of your eyebrows. They're black and lustrous, but by leaving them straggly they're a blemish. They'd be beautiful if you'd take care of them in one-tenth the time you take doing nothing. You're going to brush them so that they'll grow straight.'

Bernice raised the brows in question.

'Do you mean to say that men notice eyebrows?'

'Yes—subconsciously. And when you go home you ought to have your teeth straightened a little. It's almost imperceptible, still——'

'But I thought,' interrupted Bernice in bewilderment, 'that you despised little dainty feminine things like that.'

'I hate dainty minds,' answered Marjorie. 'But a girl has to be dainty in person. If she looks like a million dollars she can talk about Russia, ping-pong, or the League of Nations and get away with it.'

'What else?'

'Oh, I'm just beginning! There's your dancing.'

'Don't I dance all right?'

'No, you don't—you lean on a man; yes, you do—ever so slightly. I noticed it when we were dancing together yesterday. And you dance standing up straight instead of bending over a little. Probably some old lady on the sideline once told you that you looked so dignified that way. But except with a very small girl it's much harder on the man, and he's the one that counts.'

'Go on.' Bernice's brain was reeling.

'Well, you've got to learn to be nice to men who are sad birds. You look as if you'd been insulted whenever you're thrown with any except the most popular boys. Why, Bernice, I'm cut in on every few feet—and who does most of it? Why, those very sad birds. No girl can afford to neglect them. They're the big part of any crowd. Young boys too shy to talk are the very best conversational practice. Clumsy boys are the best dancing practice. If you can follow them and yet look graceful you can follow a baby tank across a barb-wire sky-scraper.'

Bernice sighed profoundly, but Marjorie was not through.

'If you go to a dance and really amuse, say, three sad birds that dance with you; if you talk so well to them that they forget they're stuck with you, you've done something. They'll come back next time, and gradually so many sad birds will dance with you that the attractive boys will see there's no danger of being stuck—then they'll dance with you.'

'Yes,' agreed Bernice faintly. 'I think I begin to see.'

'And finally,' concluded Marjorie, 'poise and charm will just come. You'll wake up some morning knowing you've attained it, and men will know it too.'

Bernice rose.

'It's been awfully kind of you—but nobody's ever talked to me like this before, and I feel sort of startled.'

Marjorie made no answer but gazed pensively at her own image in the mirror.

'You're a peach to help me,' continued Bernice.

Still Marjorie did not answer, and Bernice thought she had seemed too grateful.

'I know you don't like sentiment,' she said timidly.

Marjorie turned to her quickly.

'Oh, I wasn't thinking about that. I was considering whether we hadn't better bob your hair.'

Bernice collapsed backward upon the bed.

IV

On the following Wednesday evening there was a dinner-dance at the country club. When the guests strolled in Bernice found her place-card with a slight feeling of irritation. Though at her right sat G. Reece Stoddard, a most desirable and distinguished young bachelor, the all-important left held only Charley Paulson. Charley lacked height, beauty, and social shrewdness, and in her new enlightenment Bernice decided that his only qualification to be her partner was that he had never been stuck with her. But this feeling of irritation left with the last of the soup-plates, and Marjorie's specific instruction came to her. Swallowing her pride she turned to Charley Paulson and plunged.

'Do you think I ought to bob my hair, Mr Charley Paulson?'

Charley looked up in surprise.

'Why?'

'Because I'm considering it. It's such a sure and easy way of attracting attention.'

Charley smiled pleasantly. He could not know this had been rehearsed. He replied that he didn't know much about bobbed hair. But Bernice was there to tell him.

'I want to be a society vampire, you see,' she announced coolly, and went on to inform him that bobbed hair was the necessary prelude. She added that she wanted to ask his advice, because she had heard he was so critical about girls.

Charley, who knew as much about the psychology of women as he did of the mental states of Buddhist contemplatives, felt vaguely flattered.

'So I've decided,' she continued, her voice rising slightly, 'that early next week I'm going down to the Sevier Hotel barber-shop, sit in the first chair, and get my hair bobbed.' She faltered, noticing that the people near her had paused in their conversation and were listening; but after a confused second Marjorie's coaching told, and she finished her paragraph to the vicinity at large. 'Of course I'm charging admission, but if you'll all come down and encourage me I'll issue passes for the inside seats.'

There was a ripple of appreciative laughter, and under cover of it G. Reece Stoddard leaned over quickly and said to her ear: 'I'll take a box right now.'

She met his eyes and smiled as if he had said something surpassingly brilliant.

'Do you believe in bobbed hair?' asked G. Reece in the same undertone.

'I think it's unmoral,' affirmed Bernice gravely. 'But, of course, you've either got to amuse people or feed 'em' or shock 'em.' Marjorie had culled this from Oscar Wilde. It was greeted with a ripple of laughter from the men and a series of quick, intent looks from the girls. And then as though she had said nothing of wit or moment Bernice turned again to Charley and spoke confidentially in his ear.

'I want to ask you your opinion of several people. I imagine you're a wonderful judge of character.'

Charley thrilled faintly—paid her a subtle compliment by overturning her water.

Two hours later, while Warren McIntyre was standing passively in the stag line abstractedly watching the dancers and wondering whither and with whom Marjorie had disappeared, an unrelated perception began to creep slowly upon him—a perception that Bernice, cousin to Marjorie, had been cut in on several times in the past five minutes. He closed his eyes, opened them and looked again. Several minutes back she had been dancing with a visiting boy, a matter easily accounted for; a visiting boy would know no better. But now she was dancing with some one else, and there was Charley Paulson headed for her with enthusiastic determination in his eye. Funny—Charley seldom danced with more than three girls an evening.

Warren was distinctly surprised when—the exchange having been effected—the man relieved proved to be none other than G. Reece Stoddard himself. And G. Reece seemed not at all jubilant at being relieved. Next time Bernice danced near, Warren regarded her intently. Yes, she was pretty, distinctly pretty; and to-night her face seemed really vivacious. She had that look that no woman, however histrionically proficient, can successfully counterfeit—she looked as if she were having a good time. He liked the way she had her hair arranged, wondering if it was brilliantine that made it glisten so. And that dress was becoming—a dark red that set off her shadowy eyes and high colouring. He remembered that he had thought her pretty when she first came to town, before he had realized that she was dull. Too bad she was dull—dull girls unbearable—certainly pretty though.

His thoughts zigzagged back to Marjorie. This disappearance would be like other disappearances. When she reappeared he would demand where she had been—would be told emphatically that it was none of his business. What a pity she was so sure of him! She basked in the knowledge that no other girl in town interested him; she defied him to fall in love with Genevieve or Roberta.

Warren sighed. The way to Marjorie's affections was a labyrinth indeed. He looked up. Bernice was again dancing with the visiting boy. Half unconsciously he took a step out from the stag line in her direction, and hesitated. Then he said to himself that it was charity. He walked towards her—collided suddenly with G. Reece Stoddard.

'Pardon me,' said Warren.

But G. Reece had not stopped to apologize. He had again cut in on Bernice.

That night at one o'clock Marjorie, with one hand on the electric-light switch in the hall, turned to take a last look at Bernice's sparkling eyes.

'So it worked?'

'Oh, Marjorie, yes!' cried Bernice.

'I saw you were having a gay time.'

'I did! The only trouble was that about midnight I ran short of talk. I had to repeat myself—with different men of course. I hope they won't compare notes.'

'Men don't,' said Marjorie, yawning, 'and it wouldn't matter if they did—they'd think you were even trickier.'

She snapped out the light, and as they started up the stairs Bernice grasped the banister thankfully. For the first time in her life she had been danced tired.

'You see,' said Marjorie at the top of the stairs, 'one man sees another man cut in and he thinks there must be something there. Well, we'll fix up some new stuff to-morrow. Good night.'

'Good night.'

As Bernice took down her hair she passed the evening before her in review. She had followed instructions exactly. Even when Charley Paulson cut in for the eighth time she had simulated delight and had apparently been both interested and flattered. She had not talked about the weather or Eau Claire or automobiles or her school, but had confined her conversation to me, you, and us.

But a few minutes before she fell asleep a rebellious thought was churning drowsily in her brain—after all, it was she who had done it. Marjorie, to be sure, had given her her conversation, but then Marjorie got much of her conversation out of things she read. Bernice had bought the red dress, though she had never valued it highly before Marjorie dug it out of her trunk—and her own voice had said the words, her own lips had smiled, her own feet had danced. Marjorie nice girl—vain, though—nice evening—nice boys—like Warren—Warren—Warren—what's-his-name—Warren——

She fell asleep.

V

To Bernice the next week was a revelation. With the feeling that people really enjoyed looking at her and listening to her came the foundation of self-confidence. Of course there were numerous mistakes at first. She did not know, for instance, that Draycott Deyo was studying for the ministry; she was unaware that he had cut in on her because he thought she was a quiet, reserved girl. Had she known these things she would not have treated him to the line which began 'Hello, Shell Shock!' and continued with the bathtub story—'It takes a frightful lot of energy to fix my hair in the summer—there's so much of it—so I always fix it first and powder my face and put on my hat; then I get into the bathtub, and dress afterwards. Don't you think that's the best plan?'

Though Draycott Deyo was in the throes of difficulties concerning baptism by immersion and might possibly have seen a connection, it must be admitted that he did not. He considered feminine bathing an immoral subject, and gave her some of his ideas on the depravity of modern society.

But to offset that unfortunate occurrence Bernice had several signal successes to her credit. Little Otis Ormonde pleaded off from a trip East and elected instead to follow her with a puppylike devotion, to the amusement of his crowd and to the irritation of G. Reece Stoddard, several of whose afternoon calls Otis completely ruined by the disgusting tenderness of the glances he bent on Bernice. He even told her the story of the two-by-four and the dressing-room to show her how frightfully mistaken he and every one else had been in their first judgment of her. Bernice laughed off that incident with a slight sinking sensation.

Of all Bernice's conversation perhaps the best known and most universally approved was the line about the bobbing of her hair.

'Oh, Bernice, when you goin' to get the hair bobbed?'

'Day after to-morrow maybe,' she would reply, laughing. 'Will you come and see me? Because I'm counting on you, you know.'

'Will we? You know! But you better hurry up.'

Bernice, whose tonsorial intentions were strictly dishonourable, would laugh again.

'Pretty soon now. You'd be surprised.'

But perhaps the most significant symbol of her success was the grey car of the hypercritical Warren McIntyre, parked daily in front of the Harvey house. At first the parlourmaid was distinctly startled when he asked for Bernice instead of Marjorie; after a week of it she told the cook that Miss Bernice had gotta hold Miss Marjorie's best fella.

And Miss Bernice had. Perhaps it began with Warren's desire to rouse jealousy in Marjorie; perhaps it was the familiar though unrecognized strain of Marjorie in Bernice's conversation; perhaps it was both of these and something of sincere attraction besides. But somehow the collective mind of the younger set knew within a week that Marjorie's most reliable beau had made an amazing face-about and was giving an indisputable rush to Marjorie's guest. The question of the moment was how Marjorie would take it. Warren called Bernice on the 'phone twice a day, sent her notes, and they were frequently seen together in his roadster, obviously engrossed in one of those tense, significant conversations as to whether or not he was sincere.

Marjorie on being twitted only laughed. She said she was mighty glad that Warren had at last found some one who appreciated him. So the younger set laughed, too, and guessed that Marjorie didn't care and let it go at that.

One afternoon when there were only three days left of her visit Bernice was waiting in the hall for Warren, with whom she was going to a bridge party. She was in rather a blissful mood, and when Marjorie—also bound for the party—appeared beside her and began casually to adjust her hat in the mirror, Bernice was utterly unprepared for anything in the nature of a clash. Marjorie did her work very coldly and succinctly in three sentences.

'You may as well get Warren out of your head,' she said coldly.

'What?' Bernice was utterly astounded.

'You may as well stop making a fool of yourself over Warren McIntyre. He doesn't care a snap of his fingers about you.'

For a tense moment they regarded each other—Marjorie scornful, aloof; Bernice astounded, half-angry, half-afraid. Then two cars drove up in front of the house and there was a riotous honking. Both of them gasped faintly, turned, and side by side hurried out.

All through the bridge party Bernice strove in vain to master a rising uneasiness. She had offended Marjorie, the sphinx of sphinxes. With the most wholesome and innocent intentions in the world she had stolen Marjorie's property. She felt suddenly and horribly guilty. After the bridge game, when they sat in an informal circle and the conversation became general, the storm gradually broke. Little Otis Ormonde inadvertently precipitated it.

'When you going back to kindergarten, Otis?' some one had asked.

'Me? Day Bernice gets her hair bobbed.'

'Then your education's over,' said Marjorie quickly.

'That's only a bluff of hers. I should think you'd have realized.'

'That a fact?' demanded Otis, giving Bernice a reproachful glance.

Bernice's ears burned as she tried to think up an effectual comeback. In the face of this direct attack her imagination was paralysed.

'There's a lot of bluffs in the world,' continued Marjorie quite pleasantly. 'I should think you'd be young enough to know that, Otis.'

'Well,' said Otis, 'maybe so. But gee! With a line like Bernice's——'

'Really?' yawned Marjorie. 'What's her latest bon mot?'

No one seemed to know. In fact, Bernice, having trifled with her muse's beau, had said nothing memorable of late.

'Was that really all a line?' asked Roberta curiously.

Bernice hesitated. She felt that wit in some form was demanded of her, but under her cousin's suddenly frigid eyes she was completely incapacitated.

'I don't know,' she stalled.

'Splush!' said Marjorie. 'Admit it!'

Bernice saw that Warren's eyes had left a ukulele he had been tinkering with and were fixed on her questioningly.

'Oh, I don't know!' she repeated steadily. Her cheeks were glowing.

'Splush!' remarked Marjorie again.

'Come through, Bernice,' urged Otis. 'Tell her where to get off.'

Bernice looked round again—she seemed unable to get away from Warren's eyes.

'I like bobbed hair,' she said hurriedly, as if he had asked her a question, 'and I intend to bob mine.'

'When?' demanded Marjorie.

'Any time.'

'No time like the present,' suggested Roberta.

Otis jumped to his feet.

'Good stuff!' he cried. 'We'll have a summer bobbing party. Sevier Hotel barber-shop, I think you said.'

In an instant all were on their feet. Bernice's heart throbbed violently.

'What?' she gasped.

Out of the group came Marjorie's voice, very clear and contemptuous.

'Don't worry—she'll back out!'

'Come on, Bernice!' cried Otis, starting towards the door.

Four eyes—Warren's and Marjorie's—stared at her, challenged her, defied her. For another second she wavered wildly.

'All right,' she said swiftly, 'I don't care if I do.'

An eternity of minutes later, riding down-town through the late afternoon beside Warren, the others following in Roberta's car close behind, Bernice had all the sensations of Marie Antoinette bound for the guillotine in a tumbrel. Vaguely she wondered why she did not cry out that it was all a mistake. It was all she could do to keep from clutching her hair with both hands to protect it from the suddenly hostile world. Yet she did neither. Even the thought of her mother was no deterrent now. This was the test supreme of her sportsmanship; her right to walk unchallenged in the starry heaven of popular girls.

Warren was moodily silent, and when they came to the hotel he drew up at the curb and nodded to Bernice to precede him out. Roberta's car emptied a laughing crowd into the shop, which presented two bold plate-glass windows to the street.

Bernice stood on the curb and looked at the sign, Sevier Barber-Ship. It was a guillotine indeed, and the hangman was the first barber, who, attired in a white coat and smoking a cigarette, leaned nonchalantly against the first chair. He must have heard of her; he must have been waiting all week, smoking eternal cigarettes beside that portentous, too-often-mentioned first chair. Would they blindfold her? No, but they would tie a white cloth round her neck lest any of her blood—nonsense—hair—should get on her clothes.

'All right, Bernice,' said Warren quickly.

With her chin in the air she crossed the sidewalk, pushed open the swinging screen-door, and giving not a glance to the uproarious, riotous row that occupied the waiting bench, went up to the first barber.

'I want you to bob my hair.'

The first barber's mouth slid somewhat open. His cigarette dropped to the floor.

'Huh?'

'My hair—bob it!'

Refusing further preliminaries, Bernice took her seat on high. A man in the chair next to her turned on his side and gave her a glance, half lather, half amazement. One barber started and spoiled little Willy Schuneman's monthly haircut. Mr O'Reilly in the last chair grunted and swore musically in ancient Gaelic as a razor bit into his cheek. Two bootblacks became wide-eyed and rushed for her feet. No, Bernice didn't care for a shine.

Outside a passer-by stopped and stared; a couple joined him; half a dozen small boys' noses sprang into life, flattened against the glass; and snatches of conversation borne on the summer breeze drifted in through the screen-door.

'Lookada long hair on a kid!'

'Where'd yuh get 'at stuff? 'At's a bearded lady he just finished shavin'.'

But Bernice saw nothing, heard nothing. Her only living sense told her that this man in the white coat had removed one tortoiseshell comb and then another; that his fingers were fumbling clumsily with unfamiliar hairpins; that this hair, this wonderful hair of hers, was going— she would never again feel its long voluptuous pull as it hung in a dark-brown glory down her back. For a second she was near breaking down, and then the picture before her swam mechanically into her vision—Marjorie's mouth curling in a faint ironic smile as if to say:

'Give up and get down! You tried to buck me and I called your bluff. You see you haven't got a prayer.'

And some last energy rose up in Bernice, for she clenched her hands under the white cloth, and there was a curious narrowing of her eyes that Marjorie remarked on to some one long afterward.

Twenty minutes later the barber swung her round to face the mirror, and she flinched at the full extent of the damage that had been wrought. Her hair was not curly, and now it lay in lank lifeless blocks on both sides of her suddenly pale face. It was ugly as sin—she had known it would be ugly as sin. Her face's chief charm had been a Madonna-like simplicity. Now that was gone and she was —well, frightfully mediocre—not stagy; only ridiculous, like a Greenwich Villager who had left her spectacles at home.

As she climbed down from the chair she tried to smile —failed miserably. She saw two of the girls exchange glances; noticed Marjorie's mouth curved in attenuated mockery—and that Warren's eyes were suddenly very cold.

'You see'—her words fell into an awkward pause—'I've done it.'

'Yes, you've—done it,' admitted Warren.

'Do you like it?'

There was a half-hearted 'Sure' from two or three voices, another awkward pause, and then Marjorie turned swiftly and with serpent-like intensity to Warren.

'Would you mind running me down to the cleaners?' she asked. 'I've simply got to get a dress there before supper. Roberta's driving right home and she can take the others.'

Warren stared abstractedly at some infinite speck out the window. Then for an instant his eyes rested coldly on Bernice before they turned to Marjorie.

'Be glad to,' he said slowly.

VI

Bernice did not fully realize the outrageous trap that had been set for her until she met her aunt's amazed glance just before dinner.

'Why, Bernice!'

'I've bobbed it, Aunt Josephine.'

'Why, child!'

'Do you like it?'

'Why, Ber-nice!'

'I suppose I've shocked you.'

'No, but what'll Mrs Deyo think to-morrow night? Bernice, you should have waited until after the Deyos' dance —you should have waited if you wanted to do that.'

'It was sudden, Aunt Josephine. Anyway, why does it matter to Mrs Deyo particularly?'

'Why, child,' cried Mrs Harvey, 'in her paper on "The Foibles of the Younger Generation" that she read at the last meeting of the Thursday Club she devoted fifteen minutes to bobbed hair. It's her pet abomination. And the dance is for you and Marjorie!'

'I'm sorry.'

'Oh, Bernice, what'll your mother say? She'll think I let you do it.'

'I'm sorry.'

Dinner was an agony. She had made a hasty attempt with a curling-iron, and burned her finger and much hair. She could see that her aunt was both worried and grieved, and her uncle kept saying, 'Well, I'll be darned!' over and over in a hurt and faintly hostile tone. And Marjorie sat very quietly, entrenched behind a faint smile, a faintly mocking smile.

Somehow she got through the evening. Three boys called; Marjorie disappeared with one of them, and Bernice made a listless unsuccessful attempt to entertain the two others—sighed thankfully as she climbed the stairs to her room at half past ten. What a day!

When she had undressed for the night the door opened and Marjorie came in.

'Bernice,' she said, 'I'm awfully sorry about the Deyo dance. I'll give you my word of honour I'd forgotten all about it.'

' 'Sall right,' said Bernice shortly. Standing before the mirror she passed her comb slowly through her short hair.

'I'll take you down-town to-morrow,' continued Marjorie, 'and the hairdresser'll fix it so you'll look slick. I didn't imagine you'd go through with it. I'm really mighty sorry.'

'Oh, 'sall right!'

'Still it's your last night, so I suppose it won't matter much.'

Then Bernice winced as Marjorie tossed her own hair over her shoulders and began to twist it slowly into two long blond braids until in her cream-coloured négligé she looked like a delicate painting of some Saxon princess. Fascinated, Bernice watched the braids grow. Heavy and luxurious they were, moving under the supple fingers like restive snakes—and to Bernice remained this relic and the curling-iron and a to-morrow full of eyes. She could see G. Reece Stoddard, who liked her, assuming his Harvard manner and telling his dinner partner that Bernice shouldn't have been allowed to go to the movies so much; she could see Draycott Deyo exchanging glances with his mother and then being conscientiously charitable to her. But then perhaps by to-morrow Mrs Deyo would have heard the news; would send round an icy little note requesting that she fail to appear—and behind her back they would all laugh and know that Marjorie had made a fool of her; that her chance at beauty had been sacrificed to the jealous whim of a selfish girl. She sat down suddenly before the mirror, biting the inside of her cheek.

'I like it,' she said with an effort. 'I think it will be becoming.'

Marjorie smiled.

'It looks all right. For heaven's sake, don't let it worry you!'

'I won't.'

'Good night, Bernice.'

But as the door closed something snapped within Bernice. She sprang dynamically to her feet, clenching her hands, then swiftly and noiselessly crossed over to her bed and from underneath it dragged out her suitcase. Into it she tossed toilet articles and a change of clothing. Then she turned to her trunk and quickly dumped in two drawerfuls of lingerie and summer dresses. She moved quietly, but with deadly efficiency, and in three-quarters of an hour her trunk was locked and strapped and she was fully dressed in a becoming new travelling suit that Marjorie had helped her pick out.

Sitting down at her desk she wrote a short note to Mrs Harvey, in which she briefly outlined her reasons for going. She sealed it, addressed it, and laid it on her pillow. She glanced at her watch. The train left at one, and she knew that if she walked down to the Marborough Hotel two blocks away she could easily get a taxicab.

Suddenly she drew in her breath sharply and an expression flashed into her eyes that a practised character reader might have connected vaguely with the set look she had worn in the barber's chair—somehow a development of it. It was quite a new look for Bernice—and it carried consequences.

She went stealthily to the bureau, picked up an article that lay there, and turning out all the lights stood quietly until her eyes became accustomed to the darkness. Softly she pushed open the door to Marjorie's room. She heard the quiet, even breathing of an untroubled conscience asleep.

She was by the bedside now, very deliberate and calm. She acted swiftly. Bending over she found one of the braids of Marjorie's hair, followed it up with her hand to the point nearest the head, and then holding it a little slack so that the sleeper would feel no pull, she reached

down with the shears and severed it. With the pigtail in
her hand she held her breath. Marjorie had muttered
something in her sleep. Bernice deftly amputated the other
braid, paused for an instant, and then flitted swiftly and
silently back to her own room.

Downstairs she opened the big front door, closed it
carefully behind her, and feeling oddly happy and exuber-
ant stepped off the porch into the moonlight, swinging her
heavy grip like a shopping-bag. After a minute's brisk walk
she discovered that her left hand still held the two blond
braids. She laughed unexpectedly—had to shut her mouth
hard to keep from emitting an absolute peal. She was
passing Warren's house now, and on the impulse she set
down her baggage, and swinging the braids like pieces
of rope flung them at the wooden porch, where they
landed with a slight thud. She laughed again, no longer
restraining herself.

'Huh!' she giggled wildly. 'Scalp the selfish thing!'

Then picking up her suitcase she set off at a half-run
down the moonlit street.

THE ICE PALACE

[1920]

THE sunlight dripped over the house like golden paint
over an art jar, and the freckling shadows here and there
only intensified the rigour of the bath of light. The Butter-
worth and Larkin houses flanking were intrenched behind
great stodgy trees; only the Happer house took the full
sun, and all day long faced the dusty road-street with a
tolerant kindly patience. This was the city of Tarleton
in southernmost Georgia, September afternoon.

Up in her bedroom window Sally Carrol Happer rested
her nineteen-year-old chin on a fifty-two-year-old sill and
watched Clark Darrow's ancient Ford turn the corner.
The car was hot—being partly metallic it retained all the
heat it absorbed or evolved—and Clark Darrow sitting
bolt upright at the wheel wore a pained, strained expression as though he considered himself a spare part, and
rather like to break. He laboriously crossed two dust
ruts, the wheels squeaking indignantly at the encounter,
and then with a terrifying expression he gave the steering-
gear a final wrench and deposited self and car approximately in front of the Happer steps. There was a plaintive
heaving sound, a death-rattle, followed by a short silence;
and then the air was rent by a startling whistle.

Sally Carrol gazed down sleepily. She started to yawn,
but finding this quite impossible unless she raised her chin
from the window-sill, changed her mind and continued
silently to regard the car, whose owner sat brilliantly if
perfunctorily at attention as he waited for an answer to
his signal. After a moment the whistle once more split the
dusty air.

'Good mawnin'.'

With difficulty Clark twisted his tall body round and bent a distorted glance on the window.

' 'Tain't mawnin', Sally Carrol.'

'Isn't it, sure enough?'

'What you doin'?'

'Eatin' 'n apple.'

'Come on go swimmin'—want to?'

'Reckon so.'

'How 'bout hurryin' up?'

'Sure enough.'

Sally Carrol sighed voluminously and raised herself with profound inertia from the floor, where she had been occupied in alternately destroying parts of a green apple and painting paper dolls for her younger sister. She approached a mirror, regarded her expression with a pleased and pleasant languor, dabbed two spots of rouge on her lips and a grain of powder on her nose, and covered her bobbed corn-coloured hair with a rose-littered sunbonnet. Then she kicked over the painting water, said, 'Oh, damn!'—but it lay—and left the room.

'How you, Clark?' she inquired a minute later as she slipped nimbly over the side of the car.

'Mighty fine, Sally Carrol.'

'Where we go swimmin'?'

'Out to Walley's Pool. Told Marylyn we'd call by an' get her an' Joe Ewing.'

Clark was dark and lean, and when on foot was rather inclined to stoop. His eyes were ominous and his expression somewhat petulant except when startlingly illuminated by one of his frequent smiles. Clark had 'a income'—just enough to keep himself in ease and his car in gasoline—and he had spent the two years since he graduated from Georgia Tech in dozing round the lazy streets of his home town, discussing how he could best invest his capital for an immediate fortune.

Hanging round he found not at all difficult; a crowd of little girls had grown up beautifully, the amazing Sally Carrol foremost among them; and they enjoyed being swum with and danced with and made love to in the flower-filled summery evenings—and they all liked Clark immensely. When feminine company palled there were half a dozen other youths who were always just about to do something, and meanwhile were quite willing to join him in a few holes of golf, or a game of billiards, or the consumption of a quart of 'hard yella licker.' Every once in a while one of these contemporaries made a farewell round of calls before going up to New York or Philadelphia or Pittsburgh to go into business, but mostly they just stayed round in this languid paradise of dreamy skies and firefly evenings and noisy niggery street fairs— and especially of gracious, soft-voiced girls, who were brought up on memories instead of money.

The Ford having been excited into a sort of restless resentful life Clark and Sally Carrol rolled and rattled down Valley Avenue into Jefferson Street, where the dust road became a pavement; along opiate Millicent Place, where there were half a dozen prosperous, substantial mansions; and on into the down-town section. Driving was perilous here, for it was shopping time; the population idled casually across the streets and a drove of low-moaning oxen were being urged along in front of a placid street-car; even the shops seemed only yawning their doors and blinking their windows in the sunshine before retiring into a state of utter and finite coma.

'Sally Carrol,' said Clark suddenly, 'it a fact that you're engaged?'

She looked at him quickly.

'Where'd you hear that?'

'Sure enough, you engaged?'

' 'At's a nice question!'

'Girl told me you were engaged to a Yankee you met up in Ashville last summer.'

Sally Carrol sighed.

'Never saw such an old town for rumours.'

'Don't marry a Yankee, Sally Carrol. We need you round here.' Sally Carrol was silent a moment.

'Clark,' she demanded suddenly, 'who on earth shall I marry?'

'I offer my services.'

'Honey, you couldn't support a wife,' she answered cheerfully. 'Anyway, I know you too well to fall in love with you.'

' 'At doesn't mean you ought to marry a Yankee,' he persisted.

'Suppose I love him?'

He shook his head.

'You couldn't. He'd be a lot different from us, every way.'

He broke off as he halted the car in front of a rambling, dilapidated house. Marylyn Wade and Joe Ewing appeared in the doorway.

' 'Lo, Sally Carrol.'

'Hi!'

'How you-all?'

'Sally Carrol,' demanded Marylyn as they started off again, 'you engaged?'

'Lawdy, where'd all this start? Can't I look at a man 'thout everybody in town engagin' me to him?'

Clark stared straight in front of him at a bolt on the clattering wind-shield.

'Sally Carrol,' he said with a curious intensity, 'don't you like us?'

'What?'

'Us down here?'

'Why, Clark, you know I do. I adore all you boys.'

'Then why you gettin' engaged to a Yankee?'

'Clark, I don't know. I'm not sure what I'll do, but—well, I want to go places and see people. I want my mind to grow. I want to live where things happen on a big scale.'

'What you mean?'

'Oh, Clark, I love you, and I love Joe here, and Ben Arrot, and you-all, but you'll—you'll——'

'We'll all be failures?'

'Yes. I don't mean only money failures, but just sort of—of ineffectual and sad, and—oh, how can I tell you?'

'You mean because we stay here in Tarleton?'

'Yes, Clark; and because you like it and never want to change things or think or go ahead.'

He nodded and she reached over and pressed his hand.

'Clark,' she said softly, 'I wouldn't change you for the world. You're sweet the way you are. The things that'll make you fail I'll love always—the living in the past, the lazy days and nights you have, and all your carelessness and generosity.'

'But you're goin' away?'

'Yes—because I couldn't ever marry you. You've a place in my heart no one else ever could have, but tied down here I'd get restless. I'd feel I was—wastin' myself. There's two sides to me, you see. There's the sleepy old side you love; an' there's a sort of energy—the feelin' that makes me do wild things. That's the part of me that may be useful somewhere, that'll last when I'm not beautiful any more.'

She broke off with characteristic suddenness and sighed, 'Oh, sweet cooky!' as her mood changed.

Half closing her eyes and tipping back her head till it rested on the seat-back she let the savoury breeze fan her eyes and ripple the fluffy curls of her bobbed hair. They were in the country now, hurrying between tangled growths of bright-green coppice and grass and tall trees that sent sprays of foliage to hang a cool welcome over the road. Here and there they passed a battered Negro cabin, its oldest white-haired inhabitant smoking a corncob pipe beside the door, and half a dozen scantily clothed pickaninnies parading tattered dolls on the wild-grown grass in front. Farther out were lazy cotton-fields, where even the workers seemed intangible shadows lent by the sun to the earth, not for toil, but to while away some age-old tradition in the golden September fields. And round the drowsy picturesqueness, over the trees and shacks and muddy rivers, flowed the heat, never hostile, only comforting, like a great warm nourishing bosom for the infant earth.

'Sally Carrol, we're here!'

'Poor chile's soun' asleep.'

'Honey, you dead at last outa sheer laziness?'

'Water, Sally Carrol! Cool water waitin' for you!'

Her eyes opened sleepily.

'Hi!' she murmured, smiling.

II

In November Harry Bellamy, tall, broad, and brisk, came down from his Northern city to spend four days. His intention was to settle a matter that had been hanging fire since he and Sally Carrol had met in Asheville, North Carolina, in midsummer. The settlement took only a quiet afternoon and an evening in front of a glowing open fire, for Harry Bellamy had everything she wanted; and, besides, she loved him—loved him with that side of her she kept especially for loving. Sally Carrol had several rather clearly defined sides.

On his last afternoon they walked, and she found their steps tending half-unconsciously towards one of her favourite haunts, the cemetery. When it came in sight, grey-white and golden-green under the cheerful late sun, she paused, irresolute, by the iron gate.

'Are you mournful by nature, Harry?' she asked with a faint smile.

'Mournful? Not I.'

'Then let's go in here. It depresses some folks, but I like it.'

They passed through the gateway and followed a path that led through a wavy valley of graves—dusty-grey and mouldy for the fifties; quaintly carved with flowers and jars for the seventies; ornate and hideous for the nineties, with fat marble cherubs lying in sodden sleep on stone pillows, and great impossible growths of nameless granite flowers. Occasionally they saw a kneeling figure with tributary flowers, but over most of the graves lay silence and withered leaves with only the fragrance that their own shadowy memories could waken in living minds.

They reached the top of a hill where they were fronted by a tall, round head-stone, freckled with dark spots of damp and half grown over with vines.

'Margery Lee,' she read; '1844–1873. Wasn't she nice? She died when she was twenty-nine. Dear Margery Lee,' she added softly. 'Can't you see her, Harry?'

'Yes, Sally Carrol.'

He felt a little hand insert itself into his.

'She was dark, I think; and she always wore her hair with a ribbon in it, and gorgeous hoop-skirts of alice blue and old rose.'

'Yes.'

'Oh, she was sweet, Harry! And she was the sort of girl born to stand on a wide, pillared porch and welcome folks in. I think perhaps a lot of men went away to war meanin' to come back to her; but maybe none of 'em ever did.'

He stooped down close to the stone, hunting for any record of marriage.

'There's nothing here to show.'

'Of course not. How could there be anything there better than just "Margery Lee," and that eloquent date?'

She drew close to him and an unexpected lump came into his throat as her yellow hair brushed his cheek.

'You see how she was, don't you, Harry?'

'I see,' he agreed gently. 'I see through your precious eyes. You're beautiful now, so I know she must have been.'

Silent and close they stood, and he could feel her shoulders trembling a little. An ambling breeze swept up the hill and stirred the brim of her floppidy hat.

'Let's go down there!'

She was pointing to a flat stretch on the other side of the hill where along the green turf were a thousand greyish-white crosses stretching in endless, ordered rows like the stacked arms of a battalion.

'Those are the Confederate dead,' said Sally Carrol simply.

They walked along and read the inscriptions, always only a name and a date, sometimes quite indecipherable.

'The last row is the saddest—see, 'way over there. Every cross has just a date on it, and the word "Unknown."'

She looked at him and her eyes brimmed with tears.

'I can't tell you how real it is to me, darling—if you don't know.'

'How you feel about it is beautiful to me.'

'No, no, it's not me, it's them—that old time that I've tried to have live in me. These were just men, unimportant evidently or they wouldn't have been "unknown"; but they died for the most beautiful thing in the world —the dead South. You see,' she continued, her voice still husky, her eyes glistening with tears, 'people have these dreams they fasten onto things, and I've always grown up with that dream. It was so easy because it was all dead and there weren't any disillusions comin' to me. I've tried in a way to live up to those past standards of noblesse oblige—there's just the last remnants of it, you know, like the roses of an old garden dying all round us—streaks of strange courtliness and chivalry in some of these boys an' stories I used to hear from a Confederate soldier who lived next door, and a few old darkies. Oh, Harry, there was something, there was something! I couldn't ever make you understand, but it was there.'

'I understand,' he assured her again quietly.

Sally Carrol smiled and dried her eyes on the tip of a handkerchief protruding from his breast pocket.

'You don't feel depressed, do you, lover? Even when I cry I'm happy here, and I get a sort of strength from it.'

Hand in hand they turned and walked slowly away. Finding soft grass she drew him down to a seat beside her with their backs against the remnants of a low broken wall.

'Wish those three old women would clear out,' he complained. 'I want to kiss you, Sally Carrol.'

'Me, too.'

They waited impatiently for the three bent figures to move off, and then she kissed him until the sky seemed to fade out and all her smiles and tears to vanish in an ecstasy of eternal seconds.

Afterwards they walked slowly back together, while on the corners twilight played at somnolent black-and-white checkers with the end of day.

'You'll be up about mid-January,' he said, 'and you've got to stay a month at least. It'll be slick. There's a winter carnival on, and if you've never really seen snow it'll be like fairy-land to you. There'll be skating and skiing and tobogganing and sleigh-riding, and all sorts of torchlight parades on snow-shoes. They haven't had one for years, so they're going to make it a knock-out.'

'Will I be cold, Harry?' she asked suddenly.

'You certainly won't. You may freeze your nose, but you won't be shivery cold. It's hard and dry, you know.'

'I guess I'm a summer child. I don't like any cold I've ever seen.'

She broke off and they were both silent for a minute.

'Sally Carrol,' he said very slowly, 'what do you say to—March?'

'I say I love you.'

'March?'

'March, Harry.'

III

All night in the Pullman it was very cold. She rang for the porter to ask for another blanket, and when he couldn't give her one she tried vainly, by squeezing down into the bottom of her berth and doubling back the bedclothes, to snatch a few hours' sleep. She wanted to look her best in the morning.

She rose at six and sliding uncomfortably into her

clothes stumbled up to the diner for a cup of coffee. The snow had filtered into the vestibules and covered the floor with a slippery coating. It was intriguing, this cold, it crept in everywhere. Her breath was quite visible and she blew into the air with a naïve enjoyment. Seated in the diner she stared out the window at white hills and valleys and scattered pines whose every branch was a green platter for a cold feast of snow. Sometimes a solitary farmhouse would fly by, ugly and bleak and lone on the white waste; and with each one she had an instant of chill compassion for the souls shut in there waiting for spring.

As she left the diner and swayed back into the Pullman she experienced a surging rush of energy and wondered if she was feeling the bracing air of which Harry had spoken. This was the North, the North—her land now!

> 'Then blow, ye winds, heigho!
> A-roving I will go,'

she chanted exultantly to herself.

'What's 'at?' inquired the porter politely.

'I said: "Brush me off."'

The long wires of the telegraph-poles doubled; two tracks ran up beside the train—three—four; came a succession of white-roofed houses, a glimpse of a trolley-car with frosted windows, streets—more streets—the city.

She stood for a dazed moment in the frosty station before she saw three fur-bundled figures descending upon her.

'There she is!'

'Oh, Sally Carrol!'

Sally Carrol dropped her bag.

'Hi!'

A faintly familiar icy-cold face kissed her, and then she was in a group of faces all apparently emitting great clouds of heavy smoke; she was shaking hands. There were Gordon, a short, eager man of thirty who looked like an amateur knocked-about model for Harry, and his wife, Myra, a listless lady with flaxen hair under a fur automobile cap. Almost immediately Sally Carrol thought of her as vaguely Scandinavian. A cheerful chauffeur adopted her bag, and amid ricochets of half-phrases, exclamations, and perfunctory listless 'my dears' from Myra, they swept each other from the station.

Then they were in a sedan bound through a crooked succession of snowy streets where dozens of little boys were hitching sleds behind grocery wagons and automobiles.

'Oh,' cried Sally Carrol, 'I want to do that! Can we, Harry?'

'That's for kids. But we might——'

'It looks like such a circus!' she said regretfully.

Home was a rambling frame house set on a white lap of snow, and there she met a big, grey-haired man of whom she approved, and a lady who was like an egg, and who kissed her—these were Harry's parents. There was a breathless indescribable hour crammed full of half-sentences, hot water, bacon and eggs and confusion; and after that she was alone with Harry in the library, asking him if she dared smoke.

It was a large room with a Madonna over the fireplace and rows upon rows of books in covers of light gold and dark gold and shiny red. All the chairs had little lace squares where one's head should rest, the couch was just comfortable, the books looked as if they had been read —some—and Sally Carrol had an instantaneous vision of the battered old library at home, with her father's huge medical books, and the oil-paintings of her three great-uncles, and the old couch that had been mended up for forty-five years and was still luxurious to dream in. This room struck her as being neither attractive nor particularly otherwise. It was simply a room with a lot of fairly expensive things in it that all looked about fifteen years old.

'What do you think of it up here?' demanded Harry eagerly. 'Does it surprise you? Is it what you expected, I mean?'

'You are, Harry,' she said quietly, and reached out her arms to him.

But after a brief kiss he seemed anxious to extort enthusiasm from her.

'The town, I mean. Do you like it? Can you feel the pep in the air?'

'Oh, Harry,' she laughed, 'you'll have to give me time. You can't just fling questions at me.'

She puffed at her cigarette with a sigh of contentment.

'One thing I want to ask you,' he began rather apologetically; 'you Southerners put quite an emphasis on family, and all that—not that it isn't quite all right, but you'll find it a little different here. I mean—you'll notice a lot of things that'll seem to you sort of vulgar display at first, Sally Carrol; but just remember that this is a three-generation town. Everybody has a father, and about half of us have grandfathers. Back of that we don't go.'

'Of course,' she murmured.

'Our grandfathers, you see, founded the place, and a lot of them had to take some pretty queer jobs while they were doing the founding. For instance, there's one woman who at present is about the social model for the town; well, her father was the first public ash man— things like that.'

'Why,' said Sally Carrol, puzzled, 'did you s'pose I was goin' to make remarks about people?'

'Not at all,' interrupted Harry; 'and I'm not apologizing for any one either. It's just that—well, a Southern girl came up here last summer and said some unfortunate things, and—oh, I just thought I'd tell you.'

Sally Carrol felt suddenly indignant—as though she had been unjustly spanked—but Harry evidently considered the subject closed, for he went on with a great surge of enthusiasm.

'It's carnival time, you know. First in ten years. And there's an ice palace they're building now that's the first they've had since eighty-five. Built out of blocks of the clearest ice they could find—on a tremendous scale.'

She rose and walking to the window pushed aside the heavy Turkish portières and looked out.

'Oh!' she cried suddenly. 'There's two little boys makin' a snow man! Harry, do you reckon I can go out an' help 'em?'

'You dream! Come here and kiss me.'

She left the window rather reluctantly.

'I don't guess this is a very kissable climate, is it? I mean, it makes you so you don't want to sit round, doesn't it?'

'We're not going to. I've got a vacation for the first week you're here, and there's a dinner-dance to-night.'

'Oh, Harry,' she confessed, subsiding in a heap, half in his lap, half in the pillows, 'I sure do feel confused. I haven't got an idea whether I'll like it or not, an' I don't know what people expect, or anythin'. You'll have to tell me, honey.'

'I'll tell you,' he said softly, 'if you'll just tell me you're glad to be here.'

'Glad—just awful glad!' she whispered, insinuating herself into his arms in her own peculiar way. 'Where you are is home for me, Harry.'

And as she said this she had the feeling for almost the first time in her life that she was acting a part.

That night, amid the gleaming candles of a dinner-party, where the men seemed to do most of the talking while the girls sat in a haughty and expensive aloofness, even Harry's presence on her left failed to make her feel at home.

'They're a good-looking crowd, don't you think?' he demanded. 'Just look round. There's Spud Hubbard, tackle at Princeton last year, and Junie Morton—he and the red-haired fellow next to him were both Yale hockey captains; Junie was in my class. Why, the best athletes in the world come from these States round here. This is a man's country, I tell you. Look at John J. Fishburn!'

'Who's he?' asked Sally Carrol innocently.

'Don't you know?'

'I've heard the name.'

'Greatest wheat man in the Northwest, and one of the greatest financiers in the country.'

She turned suddenly to a voice on her right.

'I guess they forgot to introduce us. My name's Roger Patton.'

'My name is Sally Carrol Happer,' she said graciously.

'Yes, I know. Harry told me you were coming.'

'You a relative?'

'No, I'm a professor.'

'Oh,' she laughed.

'At the university. You're from the South, aren't you?'

'Yes; Tarleton, Georgia.'

She liked him immediately—a reddish-brown moustache under watery blue eyes that had something in them that these other eyes lacked, some quality of appreciation. They exchanged stray sentences through dinner, and she made up her mind to see him again.

After coffee she was introduced to numerous good-looking young men who danced with conscious precision and seemed to take it for granted that she wanted to talk about nothing except Harry.

'Heavens,' she thought, 'they talk as if my being engaged made me older than they are—as if I'd tell their mothers on them!'

In the South an engaged girl, even a young married woman, expected the same amount of half-affectionate badinage and flattery that would be accorded a débutante, but here all that seemed banned. One young man, after getting well started on the subject of Sally Carrol's eyes, and how they had allured him ever since she entered the room, went into a violent confusion when he found she was visiting the Bellamys—was Harry's fiancée. He seemed to feel as though he had made some risqué and inexcusable blunder, became immediately formal, and left her at the first opportunity.

She was rather glad when Roger Patton cut in on her and suggested that they sit out a while.

'Well,' he inquired, blinking cheerily, 'how's Carmen from the South?'

'Mighty fine. How's—how's Dangerous Dan McGrew? Sorry, but he's the only Northerner I know much about.'

He seemed to enjoy that.

'Of course,' he confessed, 'as a professor of literature I'm not supposed to have read Dangerous Dan McGrew.'

'Are you a native?'

'No, I'm a Philadelphian. Imported from Harvard to teach French. But I've been here ten years.'

'Nine years, three hundred an' sixty-four days longer than me.'

'Like it here?'

'Uh-huh. Sure do!'

'Really?'

'Well, why not? Don't I look as if I were havin' a good time?'

'I saw you look out the window a minute ago—and shiver.'

'Just my imagination,' laughed Sally Carrol. 'I'm used to havin' everythin' quiet outside, an' sometimes I look out an' see a flurry of snow, an' it's just as if somethin' dead was movin'.'

He nodded appreciatively.

'Ever been North before?'

'Spent two Julys in Asheville, North Carolina.'

'Nice-looking crowd, aren't they?' suggested Patton, indicating the swirling floor.

Sally Carrol started. This had been Harry's remark.

'Sure are! They're—canine.'

'What?'

She flushed.

'I'm sorry; that sounded worse than I meant it. You see I always think of people as feline or canine, irrespective of sex.'

'Which are you?'

'I'm feline. So are you. So are most Southern men an' most of these girls here.'

'What's Harry?'

'Harry's canine distinctly. All the men I've met to-night seem to be canine.'

'What does "canine" imply? A certain conscious masculinity as opposed to subtlety?'

'Reckon so. I never analysed it—only I just look at people an' say 'canine' or 'feline' right off. It's right absurd, I guess.'

'Not at all. I'm interested. I used to have a theory about these people. I think they're freezing up.'

'What?'

'I think they're growing like Swedes—Ibsenesque, you know. Very gradually getting gloomy and melancholy. It's these long winters. Ever read any Ibsen?'

She shook her head.

'Well, you find in his characters a certain brooding rigidity. They're righteous, narrow, and cheerless, without infinite possibilities for great sorrow or joy.'

'Without smiles or tears?'

'Exactly. That's my theory. You see there are thousands of Swedes up here. They come, I imagine, because the climate is very much like their own, and there's been a gradual mingling. There're probably not half a dozen here to-night, but—we've had four Swedish governors. Am I boring you?'

'I'm mighty interested.'

'Your future sister-in-law is half Swedish. Personally I like her, but my theory is that Swedes react rather badly on us as a whole. Scandinavians, you know, have the largest suicide rate in the world.'

'Why do you live here if it's so depressing?'

'Oh, it doesn't get me. I'm pretty well cloistered, and I suppose books mean more than people to me anyway.'

'But writers all speak about the South being tragic. You know—Spanish señoritas, black hair and daggers an' haunting music.'

He shook his head.

'No, the Northern races are the tragic races—they don't indulge in the cheering luxury of tears.'

Sally Carrol thought of her graveyard. She supposed that that was vaguely what she had meant when she said it didn't depress her.

'The Italians are about the gayest people in the world—but it's a dull subject,' he broke off. 'Anyway, I want to tell you you're marrying a pretty fine man.'

Sally Carol was moved by an impulse of confidence.

'I know. I'm the sort of person who wants to be taken care of after a certain point, and I feel sure I will be.'

'Shall we dance? You know,' he continued as they rose, 'it's encouraging to find a girl who knows what she's marrying for. Nine-tenths of them think of it as a sort of walking into a moving-picture sunset.'

She laughed, and liked him immensely.

Two hours later on the way home she nestled near Harry in the back seat.

'Oh, Harry,' she whispered, 'it's so co-old!'

'But it's warm in here, darling girl.'

'But outside it's cold; and oh, that howling wind!'

She buried her face deep in his fur coat and trembled involuntarily as his cold lips kissed the tip of her ear.

IV

The first week of her visit passed in a whirl. She had her promised toboggan-ride at the back of an automobile through a chill January twilight. Swathed in furs she put in a morning tobogganing on the country-club hill; even tried skiing, to sail through the air for a glorious moment and then land in a tangled laughing bundle on a soft snow-drift. She liked all the winter sports, except an afternoon spent snow-shoeing over a glaring plain under pale yellow sunshine, but she soon realized that these things were for children—that she was being humoured and that the enjoyment round her was only a reflection of her own.

At first the Bellamy family puzzled her. The men were

5+s.f.

reliable and she liked them; to Mr Bellamy especially, with
his iron-grey hair and energetic dignity, she took an
immediate fancy, once she found that he was born in
Kentucky; this made him a link between the old life and
the new. But towards the women she felt a definite hos-
tility. Myra, her future sister-in-law, seemed the essence of
spiritless conventionality. Her conversation was so utterly
devoid of personality that Sally Carrol, who came from a
country where a certain amount of charm and assurance
could be taken for granted in the women, was inclined to
despise her.

'If those women aren't beautiful,' she thought, 'they're
nothing. They just fade out when you look at them.
They're glorified domestics. Men are the centre of every
mixed group.'

Lastly there was Mrs Bellamy, whom Sally Carrol detested. The first day's impression of an egg had been
confirmed—an egg with a cracked, veiny voice and such an
ungracious dumpiness of carriage that Sally Carrol felt
that if she once fell she would surely scramble. In addition,
Mrs Bellamy seemed to typify the town in being innately
hostile to strangers. She called Sally Carrol 'Sally,' and
could not be persuaded that the double name was anything
more than a tedious ridiculous nickname. To Sally Carrol
this shortening of her name was like presenting her to the
public half clothed. She loved 'Sally Carrol'; she loathed
'Sally.' She knew also that Harry's mother disapproved of
her bobbed hair; and she had never dared smoke downstairs after that first day when Mrs Bellamy had come
into the library sniffing violently.

Of all the men she met she preferred Roger Patton,
who was a frequent visitor at the house. He never again
alluded to the Ibsenesque tendency of the populace, but
when he came in one day and found her curled upon the
sofa bent over 'Peer Gynt' he laughed and told her to
forget what he'd said—that it was all rot.

And then one afternoon in her second week she and
Harry hovered on the edge of a dangerously steep quarrel.

She considered that he precipitated it entirely, though the Serbia in the case was an unknown man who had not had his trousers pressed.

They had been walking homeward between mounds of high-piled snow and under a sun which Sally Carrol scarcely recognized. They passed a little girl done up in grey wool until she resembled a small Teddy bear, and Sally Carrol could not resist a gasp of maternal appreciation.

'Look! Harry!'

'What?'

'That little girl—did you see her face?'

'Yes, why?'

'It was red as a little strawberry. Oh, she was cute!'

'Why, your own face is almost as red as that already! Everybody's healthy here. We're out in the cold as soon as we're old enough to walk. Wonderful climate!'

She looked at him and had to agree. He was mighty healthy-looking; so was his brother. And she had noticed the new red in her own cheeks that very morning.

Suddenly their glances were caught and held, and they stared for a moment at the street-corner ahead of them. A man was standing there, his knees bent, his eyes gazing upward with a tense expression as though he were about to make a leap towards the chilly sky. And then they both exploded into a shout of laughter, for coming closer they discovered it had been a ludicrous momentary illusion produced by the extreme bagginess of the man's trousers.

'Reckon that's one on us,' she laughed.

'He must be a Southerner, judging by those trousers,' suggested Harry mischievously.

'Why, Harry!'

Her surprised look must have irritated him.

'Those damn Southerners!'

Sally Carrol's eyes flashed.

'Don't call 'em that!'

'I'm sorry, dear,' said Harry, malignantly apologetic, 'but you know what I think of them. They're sort of—

sort of degenerates—not at all like the old Southerners.
They've lived so long down there with all the coloured
people that they've gotten lazy and shiftless.'

'Hush your mouth, Harry!' she cried angrily. 'They're
not! They may be lazy—anybody would be in that climate
—but they're my best friends, an' I don't want to hear
'em criticised in any such sweepin' way. Some of 'em
are the finest men in the world.'

'Oh, I know. They're all right when they come North
to college, but of all the hangdog, ill-dressed, slovenly lot
I ever saw, a bunch of small-town Southerners are the
worst!'

Sally Carrol was clenching her gloved hands and biting
her lip furiously.

'Why,' continued Harry, 'there was one in my class at
New Haven, and we all thought that at last we'd found the
true type of Southern aristocrat, but it turned out that he
wasn't an aristocrat at all—just the son of a Northern
carpetbagger, who owned about all the cotton round
Mobile.'

'A Southerner wouldn't talk the way you're talking
now,' she said evenly.

'They haven't the energy!'

'Or the somethin' else.'

'I'm sorry, Sally Carrol, but I've heard you say yourself
that you'd never marry——'

'That's quite different. I told you I wouldn't want to
tie my life to any of the boys that are round Tarleton
now, but I never made any sweepin' generalities.'

They walked along in silence.

'I probably spread it on a bit thick, Sally Carrol. I'm
sorry.'

She nodded but made no answer. Five minutes later
as they stood in the hallway she suddenly threw her arms
round him.

'Oh, Harry,' she cried, her eyes brimming with tears,
'let's get married next week. I'm afraid of having fusses

like that. I'm afraid, Harry. It wouldn't be that way if we were married.'

But Harry, being in the wrong, was still irritated.

'That'd be idiotic. We decided on March.'

The tears in Sally Carrol's eyes faded; her expression hardened slightly.

'Very well—I suppose I shouldn't have said that.'

Harry melted.

'Dear little nut!' he cried. 'Come and kiss me and let's forget.'

That very night at the end of a vaudeville performance the orchestra played 'Dixie' and Sally Carrol felt something stronger and more enduring than tears and smiles of the day brim up inside her. She leaned forward gripping the arms of her chair until her face grew crimson.

'Sort of get you, dear?' whispered Harry.

But she did not hear him. To the spirited throb of the violins and the inspiring beat of the kettledrums her own old ghosts were marching by and on into the darkness, and as fifes whistled and sighed in the low encore they seemed so nearly out of sight that she could have waved good-bye.

> 'Away, away,
>   Away down South in Dixie!
> Away, away,
>   Away down South in Dixie!'

V

It was a particularly cold night. A sudden thaw had nearly cleared the streets the day before, but now they were traversed again with a powdery wraith of loose snow that travelled in wavy lines before the feet of the wind, and filled the lower air with a fine-particled mist. There was no sky—only a dark, ominous tent that draped in the tops of the streets and was in reality a vast approaching army of snowflakes—while over it all, chilling away the comfort from the brown-and-green glow of lighted windows and muffling the steady trot of the horse pulling their sleigh, interminably washed the north wind. It was a dismal town after all, she thought—dismal.

Sometimes at night it had seemed to her as though no one lived here—they had all gone long ago—leaving lighted houses to be covered in time by tombing heaps of sleet. Oh, if there should be snow on her grave! To be beneath great piles of it all winter long, where even her headstone would be a light shadow against light shadows. Her grave—a grave that should be flower-strewn and washed with sun and rain.

She thought again of those isolated country houses that her train had passed, and of the life there the long winter through—the ceaseless glare through the windows, the crust forming on the soft drifts of snow, finally the slow, cheerless melting, and the harsh spring of which Roger Patton had told her. Her spring—to lose it for ever—with its lilacs and the lazy sweetness it stirred in her heart. She was laying away that spring—afterwards she would lay away that sweetness.

With a gradual insistence the storm broke. Sally Carrol felt a film of flakes melt quickly on her eyelashes, and Harry reached over a furry arm and drew down her complicated flannel cap. Then the small flakes came in skirmish-line, and the horse bent his neck patiently as a transparency of white appeared momentarily on his coat.

'Oh, he's cold, Harry,' she said quickly.

'Who? The horse? Oh, no, he isn't. He likes it!'

After another ten minutes they turned a corner and came in sight of their destination. On a tall hill outlined in vivid glaring green against the wintry sky stood the ice palace. It was three stories in the air, with battlements and embrasures and narrow icicled windows, and the innumerable electric lights inside made a gorgeous transparency of the great central hall. Sally Carrol clutched Harry's hand under the fur robe.

'It's beautiful!' he cried excitedly. 'My golly, it's beautiful, isn't it! They haven't had one here since eighty-five!'

Somehow the notion of there not having been one since eighty-five oppressed her. Ice was a ghost, and this mansion of it was surely peopled by those shades of the eighties, with pale faces and blurred snow-filled hair.

'Come on, dear,' said Harry.

She followed him out of the sleigh and waited while he hitched the horse. A party of four—Gordon, Myra, Roger Patton, and another girl—drew up beside them with a mighty jingle of bells. There were quite a crowd already, bundled in fur or sheepskin, shouting and calling to each other as they moved through the snow, which was now so thick that people could scarcely be distinguished a few yards away.

'It's a hundred and seventy feet tall,' Harry was saying to a muffled figure beside him as they trudged towards the entrance; 'covers six thousand square yards.'

She caught snatches of conversation: 'One main hall'—'walls twenty to forty inches thick'—'and the ice cave has almost a mile of—'—'this Canuck who built it——'

They found their way inside, and dazed by the magic of the great crystal walls Sally Carrol found herself repeating over and over two lines from 'Kubla Khan':

'It was a miracle of rare device,
A sunny pleasure-dome with caves of ice!'

In the great glittering cavern with the dark shut out she took a seat on a wooden bench, and the evening's oppression lifted. Harry was right—it was beautiful; and her gaze travelled the smooth surface of the walls, the blocks for which had been selected for their purity and clearness to obtain this opalescent, translucent effect.

'Look! Here we go—oh, boy!' cried Harry.

A band in a far corner struck up: 'Hail, Hail, the Gang's All Here!' which echoed over to them in wild muddled acoustics, and then the lights suddenly went out; silence seemed to flow down the icy sides and sweep over them. Sally Carrol could still see her white breath in the darkness, and a dim row of pale faces over the other side.

The music eased to a sighing complaint, and from outside drifted in the full-throated resonant chant of the marching clubs. It grew louder like some pæan of a viking tribe traversing an ancient wild; it swelled—they were coming nearer; then a row of torches appeared, and another and another, and keeping time with their moccasined feet a long column of grey-mackinawed figures swept in, snowshoes slung at their shoulders, torches soaring and flickering as their voices rose along the great walls.

The grey column ended and another followed, the light streaming luridly this time over red toboggan caps and flaming crimson mackinaws, and as they entered they took up the refrain; then came a long platoon of blue and white, of green, of white, of brown and yellow.

'Those white ones are the Wacouta Club,' whispered Harry eagerly. 'Those are the men you've met round at dances.'

The volume of the voices grew; the great cavern was a phantasmagoria of torches waving in great banks of fire, of colours and the rhythm of soft-leather steps. The leading column turned and halted, platoon deployed in front of platoon until the whole procession made a solid flag of flame, and then from thousands of voices burst a mighty shout that filled the air like a crash of thunder, and sent the torches wavering. It was magnificent, it was tremendous! To Sally Carrol it was the North offering sacrifice on some mighty altar to the grey pagan God of Snow. As the shout died the band struck up again and there came more singing, and then long reverberating cheers by each club. She sat very quiet listening while the staccato cries rent the stillness; and then she started, for there was a volley of explosion, and great clouds of smoke went up here and there through the cavern—the flashlight photographers at work—and the council was over. With the band at their head the clubs formed in column once more, took up their chant, and began to march out.

'Come on!' shouted Harry. 'We want to see the labyrinths downstairs before they turn the lights off!'

They all rose and started towards the chute—Harry and Sally Carrol in the lead, her little mitten buried in his big fur gauntlet. At the bottom of the chute was a long empty room of ice, with the ceiling so low that they had to stoop —and their hands were parted. Before she realized what he intended Harry had darted down one of the half-dozen glittering passages that opened into the room and was only a vague receding blot against the green shimmer.

'Harry!' she called.

'Come on!' he cried back.

She looked round the empty chamber; the rest of the party had evidently decided to go home, were already outside somewhere in the blundering snow. She hesitated and then darted in after Harry.

'Harry!' she shouted.

She had reached a turning-point thirty feet down; she heard a faint muffled answer far to the left, and with a touch of panic fled towards it. She passed another turning, two more yawning alleys.

'Harry!'

No answer. She started to run straight forward, and then turned like lightning and sped back the way she had come, enveloped in a sudden icy terror.

She reached a turn—was it here?—took the left and came to what should have been the outlet into the long, low room, but it was only another glittering passage with darkness at the end. She called again but the walls gave back a flat, lifeless echo with reverberations. Retracing her steps she turned another corner, this time following a wide passage. It was like the green lane between the parted waters of the Red Sea, like a damp vault connecting empty tombs.

She slipped a little now as she walked, for ice had formed on the bottom of her overshoes; she had to run her gloves along the half-slippery, half-sticky walls to keep her balance.

'Harry!'

5*

Still no answer. The sound she made bounced mockingly down to the end of the passage.

Then on an instant the lights went out, and she was in complete darkness. She gave a small, frightened cry, and sank down into a cold little heap on the ice. She felt her left knee do something as she fell, but she scarcely noticed it as some deep terror far greater than any fear of being lost settled upon her. She was alone with this presence that came out of the North, the dreary loneliness that rose from ice-bound whalers in the Arctic seas, from smokeless, trackless wastes where were strewn the whitened bones of adventure. It was an icy breath of death; it was rolling down low across the land to clutch at her.

With a furious, despairing energy she rose again and started blindly down the darkness. She must get out. She might be lost in here for days, freeze to death and lie embedded in the ice like corpses she had read of, kept perfectly preserved until the melting of a glacier. Harry probably thought she had left with the others—he had gone by now; no one would know until late next day. She reached pitifully for the wall. Forty inches thick, they had said—forty inches thick!

'Oh!'

On both sides of her along the walls she felt things creeping, damp souls that haunted this palace, this town, this North.

'Oh, send somebody—send somebody!' she cried aloud.

Clark Darrow—he would understand; or Joe Ewing; she couldn't be left here to wander for ever—to be frozen, heart, body, and soul. This her—this Sally Carrol! Why, she was a happy thing. She was a happy little girl. She liked warmth and summer and Dixie. These things were foreign—foreign.

'You're not crying,' something said aloud. 'You'll never cry any more. Your tears would just freeze; all tears freeze up here!'

She sprawled full length on the ice.

'Oh, God!' she faltered.

A long single file of minutes went by, and with a great weariness she felt her eyes closing. Then some one seemed to sit down near her and take her face in warm, soft hands. She looked up gratefully.

'Why, it's Margery Lee,' she crooned softly to herself. 'I knew you'd come.' It really was Margery Lee, and she was just as Sally Carrol had known she would be, with a young, white brow, and wide, welcoming eyes, and a hoop-skirt of some soft material that was quite comforting to rest on.

'Margery Lee.'

It was getting darker now and darker—all those tomb-stones ought to be repainted, sure enough, only that would spoil 'em, of course. Still, you ought to be able to see 'em.

Then after a succession of moments that went fast and then slow, but seemed to be ultimately resolving them-selves into a multitude of blurred rays converging towards a pale-yellow sun, she heard a great cracking noise break her new-found stillness.

It was the sun, it was a light; a torch, and a torch beyond that, and another one, and voices; a face took flesh below the torch, heavy arms raised her, and she felt something on her cheek—it felt wet. Some one had seized her and was rubbing her face with snow. How ridiculous—with snow!

'Sally Carrol! Sally Carrol!'

It was Dangerous Dan McGrew; and two other faces she didn't know.

'Child, child! We've been looking for you two hours! Harry's half-crazy!'

Things came rushing back into place—the singing, the torches, the great shout of the marching clubs. She squirmed in Patton's arms and gave a long low cry.

'Oh, I want to get out of here! I'm going back home. Take me home'—her voice rose to a scream that sent a chill to Harry's heart as he came racing down the next passage—'to-morrow!' she cried with delirious, unre-strained passion—'To-morrow! To-morrow! To-morrow!'

VI

The wealth of golden sunlight poured a quite enervating yet oddly comforting heat over the house where day long it faced the dusty stretch of road. Two birds were making a great to-do in a cool spot found among the branches of a tree next door, and down the street a coloured woman was announcing herself melodiously as a purveyor of strawberries. It was April afternoon.

Sally Carol Happer, resting her chin on her arm, and her arm on an old window-seat gazed sleepily down over the spangled dust whence the heat waves were rising for the first time this spring. She was watching a very ancient Ford turn a perilous corner and rattle and groan to a jolting stop at the end of the walk. She made no sound, and in a minute a strident familiar whistle rent the air. Sally Carrol smiled and blinked.

'Good mawnin'.'

A head appeared tortuously from under the car-top below.

' 'Tain't mawnin', Sally Carrol.'

'Sure enough!' she said in affected surprise. 'I guess maybe not.'

'What you doin'?'

'Eatin' green peach. 'Spect to die any minute.'

Clark twisted himself a last impossible notch to get a view of her face.

'Water's warm as a kettla steam, Sally Carroll. Wanta go swimmin'?'

'Hate to move,' sighed Sally Carrol lazily, 'but I reckon so.'

MAY DAY

[1920]

THERE had been a war fought and won and the great city
of the conquering people was crossed with triumphal arches
and vivid with thrown flowers of white, red, and rose. All
through the long spring days the returning soldiers marched
up the chief highway behind the strump of drums and the
joyous, resonant wind of the brasses, while merchants and
clerks left their bickerings and figurings and, crowding to
the windows, turned their white-bunched faces gravely
upon the passing battalions.

Never had there been such splendour in the great
city, for the victorious war had brought plenty in its
train, and the merchants had flocked thither from the
South and West with their households to taste of all
the luscious feasts and witness the lavish entertainments
prepared—and to buy for their women furs against the
next winter and bags of golden mesh and varicoloured
slippers of silk and silver and rose satin and cloth of
gold.

So gaily and noisily were the peace and prosperity
impending hymned by the scribes and poets of the conquering people that more and more spenders had gathered from
the provinces to drink the wine of excitement, and faster
and faster did the merchants dispose of their trinkets and
slippers until they sent up a mighty cry for more trinkets
and more slippers in order that they might give in barter
what was demanded of them. Some even of them flung up
their hands helplessly, shouting:

'Alas! I have no more slippers! and alas! I have no more

trinkets! May Heaven help me, for I know not what I shall do!'

But no one listened to their great outcry, for the throngs were far too busy—day by day, the foot-soldiers trod jauntily the highway and all exulted because the young men returning were pure and brave, sound of tooth and pink of cheek, and the young women of the land were virgins and comely both of face and of figure.

So during all this time there were many adventures that happened in the great city, and, of these, several—or perhaps one—are here set down.

I

At nine o'clock on the morning of the first of May, 1919, a young man spoke to the room clerk at the Biltmore Hotel, asking if Mr Philip Dean were registered there, and if so, could he be connected with Mr Dean's rooms. The inquirer was dressed in a well-cut shabby suit. He was small, slender, and darkly handsome; his eyes were framed above with unusually long eyelashes and below with the blue semi-circle of ill health, this latter effect heightened by an unnatural glow which coloured his face like a low, incessant fever.

Mr Dean was staying there. The young man was directed to a telephone at the side.

After a second his connection was made; a sleepy voice hello'd from somewhere above.

'Mr Dean?'—this very eagerly—'it's Gordon, Phil. It's Gordon Sterrett. I'm downstairs. I heard you were in New York and I had a hunch you'd be here.'

The sleepy voice became gradually enthusiastic. Well, how was Gordy, old boy! Well, he certainly was surprised and tickled! Would Gordy come right up, for Pete's sake!

A few minutes later Philip Dean, dressed in blue silk pyjamas, opened his door and the two young men greeted each other with a half-embarrassed exuberance. They were both about twenty-four, Yale graduates of the year before the war; but there the resemblance stopped abruptly. Dean

was blond, ruddy, and rugged under his thin pyjamas.
Everything about him radiated fitness and bodily comfort.
He smiled frequently, showing large and prominent teeth.

'I was going to look you up,' he cried enthusiastically.
'I'm taking a couple of weeks off. If you'll sit down a sec
I'll be right with you. Going to take a shower.'

As he vanished into the bathroom his visitor's dark eyes
roved nervously around the room, resting for a moment on
a great English travelling bag in the corner and on a family
of thick silk shirts littered on the chairs amid impressive
neckties and soft woollen socks.

Gordon rose and, picking up one of the shirts, gave it a
minute examination. It was of very heavy silk, yellow with
a pale blue stripe—and there were nearly a dozen of them.
He stared involuntarily at his own shirt-cuffs—they were
ragged and linty at the edges and soiled to a faint grey.
Dropping the silk shirt, he held his coat-sleeves down and
worked the frayed shirt-cuffs up till they were out of sight.
Then he went to the mirror and looked at himself with
listless, unhappy interest. His tie, of former glory, was faded
and thumb-creased—it served no longer to hide the jagged
buttonholes of his collar. He thought, quite without amusement, that only three years before he had received a
scattering vote in the senior elections at college for being the
best-dressed man in his class.

Dean emerged from the bathroom polishing his body.

'Saw an old friend of yours last night,' he remarked.

'Passed her in the lobby and couldn't think of her name
to save my neck. That girl you brought up to New Haven
senior year.'

Gordon started.

'Edith Bradin? That whom you mean?'

''At's the one. Damn good looking. She's still sort of a
pretty doll—you know what I mean: as if you touched her
she'd smear.'

He surveyed his shining self complacently in the mirror,
smiled faintly, exposing a section of teeth.

'She must be twenty-three anyway,' he continued.

'Twenty-two last month,' said Gordon absently.

'What? Oh, last month. Well, I imagine she's down for the Gamma Psi dance. Did you know we're having a Yale Gamma Psi dance tonight at Delmonico's? You better come up, Gordy. Half of New Haven'll probably be there. I can get you an invitation.'

Draping himself reluctantly in fresh underwear, Dean lit a cigarette and sat down by the open window, inspecting his calves and knees under the morning sunshine which poured into the room.

'Sit down, Gordy,' he suggested, 'and tell me all about what you've been doing and what you're doing now and everything.'

Gordon collapsed unexpectedly upon the bed; lay there inert and spiritless. His mouth, which habitually dropped a little open when his face was in repose, became suddenly helpless and pathetic.

'What's the matter?' asked Dean quickly.

'Oh, God!'

'What's the matter?'

'Every God damn thing in the world,' he said miserably. 'I've absolutely gone to pieces, Phil. I'm all in.'

'Huh?'

'I'm all in.' His voice was shaking.

Dean scrutinized him more closely with appraising blue eyes.

'You certainly look all shot.'

'I am. I've made a hell of mess of everything.' He paused. 'I'd better start at the beginning—or will it bore you?'

'Not at all; go on.' There was, however, a hesitant note in Dean's voice. This trip East had been planned for a holiday—to find Gordon Sterrett in trouble exasperated him a little.

'Go on,' he repeated, and then added half under his breath, 'Get it over with.'

'Well,' began Gordon unsteadily, 'I got back from France in February, went home to Harrisburg for a month, and then came down to New York to get a job—one with an export company. They fired me yesterday.'

'Fired you?'

'I'm coming to that, Phil. I want to tell you frankly. You're about the only man I can turn to in a matter like this. You won't mind if I just tell you frankly, will you, Phil?'

Dean stiffened a bit more. The pats he was bestowing on his knees grew perfunctory. He felt vaguely that he was being unfairly saddled with responsibility; he was not even sure he wanted to be told. Though never surprised at finding Gordon Sterrett in mild difficulty, there was something in this present misery that repelled him and hardened him, even though it excited his curiosity.

'Go on.'

'It's a girl.'

'Hm.' Dean resolved that nothing was going to spoil his trip. If Gordon was going to be depressing, then he'd have to see less of Gordon.

'Her name is Jewel Hudson,' went on the distressed voice from the bed. 'She used to be "pure", I guess, up to about a year ago. Lived here in New York—poor family. Her people are dead now and she lives with an old aunt. You see it was just about the time I met her that everybody began to come back from France in droves—and all I did was to welcome the newly arrived and go on parties with 'em. That's the way it started, Phil, just from being glad to see everybody and having them glad to see me.'

'You ought to've had more sense.'

'I know,' Gordon paused, and then continued listlessly. 'I'm on my own now, you know, and Phil, I can't stand being poor. Then came this darn girl. She sort of fell in love with me for a while and, though I never intended to get so involved, I'd always seem to run into her somewhere. You can imagine the sort of work I was doing for those exporting people—of course, I always intended to draw; do illustrating magazines; there's a pile of money in it.'

'Why didn't you? You've got to buckle down if you want to make good,' suggested Dean with cold formalism.

'I tried, a little, but my stuff's crude. I've got talent,
Phil; I can draw—but I just don't know how. I ought to go
to art school and I can't afford it. Well, things came to a
crisis about a week ago. Just as I was down to about my last
dollar this girl began bothering me. She wants some money;
claims she can make trouble for me if she doesn't get it.'

'Can she?'

'I'm afraid she can. That's one reason I lost my job—
she kept calling up the office all the time, and that was sort
of the last straw down there. She's got a letter all written to
send to my family. Oh, she's got me, all right. I've got to
have some money for her.'

There was an awkward pause. Gordon lay very still, his
hands clenched by his side.

'I'm all in,' he continued, his voice trembling. 'I'm half
crazy, Phil. If I hadn't known you were coming East, I think
I'd have killed myself. I want you to lend me three hundred
dollars.'

Dean's hands, which had been patting his bare ankles,
were suddenly quiet—and the curious uncertainty playing
between the two became taut and strained.

After a second Gordon continued:

'I've bled the family until I'm ashamed to ask for another
nickel.'

Still Dean made no answer.

'Jewel says she's got to have two hundred dollars.'

'Tell her where she can go.'

'Yes, that sounds easy, but she's got a couple of drunken
letters I wrote her. Unfortunately she's not at all the flabby
sort of person you'd expect.'

Dean made an expression of distaste.

'I can't stand that sort of woman. You ought to have kept
away.'

'I know,' admitted Gordon wearily.

'You've got to look at things as they are. If you haven't
got money you've got to work and stay away from women.'

'That's easy for you to say,' began Gordon, his eyes
narrowing. 'You've got all the money in the world.'

'I most certainly have not. My family keep darn close tab on what I spend. Just because I have a little leeway I have to be extra careful not to abuse it.'

He raised the blind and let in a further flood of sunshine.

'I'm no prig, Lord knows,' he went on deliberately. 'I like pleasure—and I like a lot of it on a vacation like this, but you're—you're in awful shape. I never heard you talk just this way before. You seem to be sort of bankrupt—morally as well as financially.'

'Don't they usually go together?'

Dean shook his head impatiently.

'There's a regular aura about you that I don't understand. It's a sort of evil.'

'It's an air of worry and poverty and sleepless nights,' said Gordon, rather defiantly.

'I don't know.'

'Oh, I admit I'm depressing. I depress myself. But, my God, Phil, a week's rest and a new suit and some ready money and I'd be like—like I was. Phil, I can draw like a streak, and you know it. But half the time I haven't had the money to buy decent drawing materials—and I can't draw when I'm tired and discouraged and all in. With a little ready money I can take a few weeks off and get started.'

'How do I know you wouldn't use it on some other woman?'

'Why rub it in?' said Gordon quietly.

'I'm not rubbing it in. I hate to see you this way.'

'Will you lend me the money, Phil?'

'I can't decide right off. That's a lot of money and it'll be darn inconvenient for me.'

'It'll be hell for me if you can't—I know I'm whining, and it's all my own fault but—that doesn't change it.'

'When could you pay it back?'

This was encouraging. Gordon considered. It was probably wisest to be frank.

'Of course, I could promise to send it back next month, but—I'd better say three months. Just as soon as I start to sell drawings.'

'How do I know you'll sell any drawings?'

A new hardness in Dean's voice sent a faint chill of doubt over Gordon. Was it possible that he wouldn't get the money?

'I supposed you had a little confidence in me.'

'I did have—but when I see you like this I begin to wonder.'

'Do you suppose if I wasn't at the end of my rope I'd come to you like this? Do you think I'm enjoying it?' He broke off and bit his lip, feeling that he had better subdue the rising anger in his voice. After all, he was the suppliant.

'You seem to manage it pretty easily,' said Dean angrily. 'You put me in the position where, if I don't lend it to you, I'm a sucker—oh, yes, you do. And let me tell you it's no easy thing for me to get hold of three hundred dollars. My income isn't so big but that a slice like that won't play the deuce with it.'

He left his chair and began to dress, choosing his clothes carefully. Gordon stretched out his arms and clenched the edges of the bed, fighting back a desire to cry out. His head was splitting and whirring, his mouth was dry and bitter and he could feel the fever in his blood resolving itself into innumerable regular counts like a slow dripping from a roof.

Dean tied his tie precisely, brushed his eyebrows, and removed a piece of tobacco from his teeth with solemnity. Next he filled his cigarette case, tossed the empty box thoughtfully into the waste basket, and settled the case in his vest pocket.

'Had breakfast?' he demanded.

'No; I don't eat it any more.'

'Well, we'll go out and have some. We'll decide about that money later. I'm sick of the subject. I came East to have a good time.

'Let's go over to the Yale Club,' he continued moodily, and then added with an implied reproof: 'You've given up your job. You've got nothing else to do.'

'I'd have a lot to do if I had a little money,' said Gordon pointedly.

'Oh, for Heaven's sake drop the subject for a while! No
point in glooming on my whole trip. Here, here's some
money.'

He took a five-dollar bill from his wallet and tossed it
over to Gordon, who folded it carefully and put it in his
pocket. There was an added spot of colour in his cheeks,
an added glow that was not fever. For an instant before they
turned to go out their eyes met and in that instant each
found something that made him lower his own glance
quickly. For in that instant they quite suddenly and
definitely hated each other.

II

Fifth Avenue and Forty-fourth Street swarmed with the
noon crowd. The wealthy, happy sun glittered in transient
gold through the thick windows of the smart shops, lighting
upon mesh bags and purses and strings of pearls in grey
velvet cases; upon gaudy feather fans of many colours;
upon the laces and silks of expensive dresses; upon the bad
paintings and the fine period furniture in the elaborate
show rooms of interior decorators.

Working-girls, in pairs and groups and swarms, loitered
by the windows, choosing their future boudoirs from some
resplendent display which included even a man's silk
pyjamas laid domestically across the bed. They stood in
front of the jewellery stores and picked out their engagement
rings, and their wedding rings and their platinum wrist
watches, and then drifted on to inspect the feather fans and
opera cloaks; meanwhile digesting the sandwiches and
sundaes they had eaten for lunch.

All through the crowd were men in uniform, sailors from
the great fleet anchored in the Hudson, soldiers with
divisional insignia from Massachusetts to California wanting
fearfully to be noticed, and finding the great city thoroughly
fed up with soldiers unless they were nicely massed into
pretty formations and uncomfortable under the weight of
a pack and rifle.

Through this medley Dean and Gordon wandered; the

former interested, made alert by the display of humanity at its frothiest and gaudiest; the latter reminded of how often he had been one of the crowd, tired, casually fed, over-worked, and dissipated. To Dean the struggle was significant, young, cheerful; to Gordon it was dismal, meaningless, endless.

In the Yale Club they met a group of their former class-mates who greeted the visiting Dean vociferously. Sitting in a semicircle of lounges and great chairs, they had a highball all around.

Gordon found the conversation tiresome and intermin-able. They lunched together *en masse*, warmed with liquor as the afternoon began. They were all going to the Gamma Psi dance that night—it promised to be the best party since the war.

'Edith Bradin's coming,' said someone to Gordon. 'Didn't she used to be an old flame of yours? Aren't you both from Harrisburg?'

'Yes.' He tried to change the subject. 'I see her brother occasionally. He's sort of a socialistic nut. Runs a paper or something here in New York.'

'Not like his gay sister, eh?' continued his eager infor-mant. 'Well, she's coming tonight with a junior named Peter Himmell.'

Gordon was to meet Jewel Hudson at eight o'clock—he had promised to have some money for her. Several times he glanced nervously at his wrist-watch. At four to his relief, Dean rose and announced that he was going over to Rivers Brothers to buy some collars and ties. But as they left the Club another of the party joined them, to Gordon's great dismay. Dean was in a jovial mood now, happy, expectant of the evening's party, faintly hilarious. Over in Rivers he chose a dozen neckties, selecting each one after long consultations with the other man. Did he think narrow ties were coming back? And wasn't it a shame that Rivers couldn't get any more Welsh Margotson collars? There never was a collar like the 'Covington.'

Gordon was in something of a panic. He wanted the

money immediately. And he was now inspired also with a vague idea of attending the Gamma Psi dance. He wanted to see Edith—Edith whom he hadn't met since one romantic night at the Harrisburg Country Club just before he went to France. The affair had died, drowned in the turmoil of the war and quite forgotten in the arabesque of these three months, but a picture of her, poignant, debonair, immersed in her own inconsequential chatter, recurred to him unexpectedly and brought a hundred memories with it. It was Edith's face that he had cherished through college with a sort of detached yet affectionate admiration. He had loved to draw her—around his room had been a dozen sketches of her—playing golf, swimming—he could draw her pert, arresting profile with his eyes shut.

They left Rivers at five-thirty and paused for a moment on the sidewalk.

'Well,' said Dean genially, 'I'm all set now. Think I'll go back to the hotel and get a shave, haircut, and massage.'

'Good enough,' said the other man, 'I think I'll join you.'

Gordon wondered if he was to be beaten after all. With difficulty he restrained himself from turning to the man and snarling out, 'Go on away, damn you!' In despair he suspected that perhaps Dean had spoken to him, was keeping him along in order to avoid a dispute about the money.

They went into the Biltmore—a Biltmore alive with girls —mostly from the West and South, the stellar débutantes of many cities gathered for the dance of a famous fraternity of a famous university. But to Gordon they were faces in a dream. He gathered together his forces for a last appeal, was about to come out with he knew not what, when Dean suddenly excused himself to the other man and taking Gordon's arm led him aside.

'Gordy,' he said quickly, 'I've thought the whole thing over carefully and I've decided that I can't lend you that money. I'd like to oblige you, but I don't feel I ought to— it'd put a crimp in me for a month.'

Gordon, watching him dully, wondered why he had never before noticed how much those upper teeth projected.

'—I'm mighty sorry, Gordon,' continued Dean, 'but that's the way it is.'

He took out his wallet and deliberately counted out seventy-five dollars in bills.

'Here,' he said, holding them out, 'here's seventy-five; that makes eighty altogether. That's all the actual cash I have with me, besides what I'll actually spend on the trip.'

Gordon raised his clenched hand automatically, opened it as though it were a tongs he was holding, and clenched it again on the money.

'I'll see you at the dance,' continued Dean. 'I've got to get along to the barber shop.'

'So-long,' said Gordon in a strained and husky voice. 'So-long.'

Dean began to smile, but seemed to change his mind. He nodded briskly and disappeared.

But Gordon stood there, his handsome face awry with distress, the roll of bills clenched tightly in his hand. Then, blinded by sudden tears, he stumbled clumsily down the Biltmore steps.

III

About nine o'clock of the same night two human beings came out of a cheap restaurant in Sixth Avenue. They were ugly, ill-nourished, devoid of all except the very lowest form of intelligence, and without even that animal exuberance that in itself brings colour into life; they were lately vermin-ridden, cold, and hungry in a dirty town of a strange land; they were poor, friendless; tossed as driftwood from their births, they would be tossed as driftwood to their deaths. They were dressed in the uniform of the United States Army, and on the shoulder of each was the insignia of a drafted division from New Jersey, landed three days before.

The taller of the two was named Carrol Key, a name hinting that in his veins, however thinly diluted by generations of degeneration, ran blood of some potentiality. But one could stare endlessly at the long, chinless face, the dull, watery eyes, and high cheek-bones, without finding a suggestion of either ancestral worth or native resourcefulness.

His companion was swart and bandy-legged, with rat-eyes and a much-broken hooked nose. His defiant air was obviously a pretence, a weapon of protection borrowed from that world of snarl and snap, of physical bluff and physical menace, in which he had always lived. His name was Gus Rose.

Leaving the café they sauntered down Sixth Avenue, wielding toothpicks with great gusto and complete detachment.

'Where to?' asked Rose, in a tone which implied that he would not be surprised if Key suggested the South Sea Islands.

'What you say we see if we can getta holda some liquor?' Prohibition was not yet. The ginger in the suggestion was caused by the law forbidding the selling of liquor to soldiers.

Rose agreed enthusiastically.

'I got an idea,' continued Key, after a moment's thought, 'I got a brother somewhere.'

'In New York?'

'Yeah. He's an old fella.' He meant that he was an elder brother. 'He's a waiter in a hash joint.'

'Maybe he can get us some.'

'I'll say he can!'

'B'lieve me, I'm goin' to get this darn uniform off me to-morra. Never get me in it again, neither. I'm goin' to get me some regular clothes.'

'Say, maybe I'm not.'

As their combined finances were something less than five dollars, this intention can be taken largely as a pleasant game of words, harmless and consoling. It seemed to please both of them, however, for they reinforced it with chuckling and mention of personages high in biblical circles, adding such further emphasis as 'Oh, boy!' 'You know!' and 'I'll say so!' repeated many times over.

The entire mental pabulum of these two men consisted of an offended nasal comment extended through the years upon the institution—army, business, or poorhouse—which kept them alive, and toward their immediate superior in that institution. Until that very morning the institution had been the 'government' and the immediate superior had been the 'Cap'n'—from these two they had glided out and were now in the vaguely uncomfortable state before they should adopt their next bondage. They were uncertain, resentful, and somewhat ill at ease. This they hid by pretending an elaborate relief at being out of the army, and by assuring each other that military discipline should never again rule their stubborn, liberty-loving wills. Yet, as a matter of fact, they would have felt more at home in a prison than in this new-found and unquestionable freedom.

Suddenly Key increased his gait. Rose, looking up and following his glance, discovered a crowd that was collecting fifty yards down the street. Key chuckled and began to run in the direction of the crowd; Rose thereupon also chuckled and his short bandy legs twinkled beside the long, awkward strides of his companion.

Reaching the outskirts of the crowd they immediately became an indistinguishable part of it. It was composed of ragged civilians somewhat the worse for liquor, and of soldiers representing many divisions and many stages of sobriety, all clustered around a gesticulating little Jew with long black whiskers, who was waving his arms and delivering an excited but succinct harangue. Key and Rose, having wedged themselves into the approximate parquet, scrutinized him with acute suspicion, as his words penetrated their common consciousness.

'—What have you got outa the war?' he was crying fiercely. 'Look arounja, look arounja! Are you rich? Have you got a lot of money offered you?—no; you're lucky if you're alive and got both your legs; you're lucky if you came back an' find your wife ain't gone off with some other fella that had the money to buy himself out of the war! That's when you're lucky! Who got anything out of it except J. P. Morgan an' John D. Rockerfeller?'

At this point the little Jew's oration was interrupted by

the hostile impact of a fist upon the point of his bearded
chin and he toppled backward to a sprawl on the pavement.

'God damn Bolsheviki!' cried the big soldier-blacksmith
who had delivered the blow. There was a rumble of
approval, the crowd closed in nearer.

The Jew staggered to his feet, and immediately went down
again before a half-dozen reaching-in fists. This time he
stayed down, breathing heavily, blood oozing from his lip
where it was cut within and without.

There was a riot of voices, and in a minute Rose and Key
found themselves flowing with the jumbled crowd down
Sixth Avenue under the leadership of a thin civilian in a
slouch hat and the brawny soldier who had summarily
ended the oration. The crowd had marvellously swollen
to formidable proportions and a stream of more non-
committal citizens followed it along the sidewalks lending
their moral support by intermittent huzzas.

'Where we goin'?' yelled Key to the man nearest him.

His neighbour pointed up to the leader in the slouch hat.

'That guy knows where there's a lot of 'em! We're goin'
to show 'em!'

'We're goin' to show 'em!' whispered Key delightedly
to Rose, who repeated the phrase rapturously to a man on
the other side.

Down Sixth Avenue swept the procession, joined here
and there by soldiers and marines, and now and then by
civilians, who came up with the inevitable cry that they were
just out of the army themselves, as if presenting it as a card of
admission to a newly formed Sporting and Amusement Club.

Then the procession swerved down a cross street and
headed for Fifth Avenue and the word filtered here and
there that they were bound for a Red meeting at Tolliver
Hall.

'Where is it?'

The question went up the line and a moment later the
answer floated back. Tolliver Hall was down on Tenth
Street. There was a bunch of other sojers who was goin'
to break it up and was down there now!

But Tenth Street had a faraway sound and at the word a general groan went up and a score of the procession dropped out. Among these were Rose and Key, who slowed down to a saunter and let the more enthusiastic sweep on by.

'I'd rather get some liquor,' said Key, as they halted and made their way to the sidewalk amid cries of 'Shell hole!' and 'Quitters!'

'Does your brother work around here?' asked Rose, assuming the air of one passing from the superficial to the eternal.

'He oughta,' replied Key. 'I ain't seen him for a coupla years. I been out to Pennsylvania since. Maybe he don't work at night anyhow. It's right along here. He can get us some o'right if he ain't gone.'

They found the place after a few minutes' patrol of the street—a shoddy tablecloth restaurant between Fifth Avenue and Broadway. Here Kay went inside to inquire for his brother, George, while Rose waited on the sidewalk.

'He ain't here no more,' said Key emerging. 'He's a waiter up to Delmonico's.'

Rose nodded wisely, as if he'd expected as much. One should not be surprised at a capable man changing jobs occasionally. He knew a waiter once—there ensued a long conversation as they walked as to whether waiters made more in actual wages than in tips—it was decided that it depended on the social tone of the joint wherein the waiter laboured. After having given each other vivid pictures of millionaires dining at Delmonico's and throwing away fifty-dollar bills after their first quart of champagne, both men thought privately of becoming waiters. In fact, Key's narrow brow was secreting a resolution to ask his brother to get him a job.

'A waiter can drink up all the champagne those fellas leave in bottles,' suggested Rose with some relish, and then added as an afterthought, 'Oh, boy!'

By the time they reached Delmonico's it was half past ten, and they were surprised to see a stream of taxis driving up to the door one after the other and emitting marvellous, hatless young ladies, each one attended by a stiff young gentleman in evening clothes.

'It's a party,' said Rose with some awe. 'Maybe we better not go in. He'll be busy.'

'No, he won't. He'll be o'right.'

After some hesitation they entered what appeared to them to be the least elaborate door and, indecision falling upon them immediately, stationed themselves nervously in an inconspicuous corner of the small dining-room in which they found themselves. They took off their caps and held them in their hands. A cloud of gloom fell upon them and both started when a door at one end of the room crashed open, emitting a comet-like waiter who streaked across the floor and vanished through another door on the other side.

There had been three of these lightning passages before the seekers mustered the acumen to hail a waiter. He turned, looked at them suspiciously, and then approached with soft, catlike steps, as if prepared at any moment to turn and flee.

'Say,' began Key, 'say, do you know my brother? He's a waiter here.'

'His name is Key,' annotated Rose.

Yes, the waiter knew Key. He was upstairs, he thought. There was a big dance going on in the main ballroom. He'd tell him.

Ten minutes later George Key appeared and greeted his brother with the utmost suspicion; his first and most natural thought being that he was going to be asked for money.

George was tall and weak chinned, but there his resemblance to his brother ceased. The waiter's eyes were not dull, they were alert and twinkling, and his manner was suave, indoor, and faintly superior. They exchanged formalities. George was married and had three children. He seemed fairly interested, but not impressed by the news that Carrol had been abroad in the army. This disappointed Carrol.

'George,' said the younger brother, these amenities having been disposed of, 'we want to get some booze, and they won't sell us none. Can you get us some?'

George considered.

'Sure. Maybe I can. It may be half an hour, though.'

'All right,' agreed Carrol, 'we'll wait.'

At this Rose started to sit down in a convenient chair, but was hailed to his feet by the indignant George.

'Hey! Watch out, you! Can't sit down here! This room's all set for a twelve o'clock banquet.'

'I ain't going to hurt it,' said Rose resentfully. 'I been through the delouser.'

'Never mind,' said George sternly, 'if the head waiter seen me here talkin' he'd romp all over me.'

'Oh.'

The mention of the head waiter was full explanation to the other two; they fingered their overseas caps nervously and waited for a suggestion.

'I tell you,' said George, after a pause, 'I got a place you can wait; you just come here with me.'

They followed him out the far door, through a deserted pantry and up a pair of dark winding stairs, emerging finally into a small room chiefly furnished by piles of pails and stacks of scrubbing brushes, and illuminated by a single dim electric light. There he left them, after soliciting two dollars and agreeing to return in half an hour with a quart of whiskey.

'George is makin' money, I bet,' said Key gloomily as he seated himself on an inverted pail. 'I bet he's making fifty dollars a week.'

Rose nodded his head and spat.

'I bet he is, too.'

'What'd he say the dance was of?'

'A lot of college fellas. Yale College.'

They both nodded solemnly at each other.

'Wonder where that crowda sojers is now?'

'I don't know. I know that's too damn long to walk for me.'

'Me too. You don't catch me walkin' that far.'

Ten minutes later restlessness seized them.

'I'm goin' to see what's out here,' said Rose, stepping cautiously towards the other door.

It was a swinging door of green baize and he pushed it open a cautious inch.

'See anything?'

For answer Rose drew in his breath sharply.

'Doggone! Here's some liquor I'll say!'

'Liquor?'

Key joined Rose at the door, and looked eagerly.

'I'll tell the world that's liquor,' he said, after a moment of concentrated gazing.

It was a room about twice as large as the one they were in —and in it was prepared a radiant feast of spirits. There were long walls of alternating bottles set along two white covered tables; whiskey, gin, brandy, French and Italian vermouths, and orange juice, not to mention an array of syphons and two great empty punch bowls. The room was as yet uninhabited.

'It's for this dance they're just starting,' whispered Key; 'hear the violins playin'? Say, boy, I wouldn't mind havin' a dance.'

They closed the door softly and exchanged a glance of mutual comprehension. There was no need of feeling each other out.

'I'd like to get my hands on a coupla those bottles,' said Rose emphatically.

'Me too.'

'Do you suppose we'd get seen?'

Key considered.

'Maybe we better wait till they start drinkin' 'em. They got 'em all laid out now, and they know how many of them there are.'

They debated this point for several minutes. Rose was all for getting his hands on a bottle now and tucking it under his coat before anyone came into the room. Key, however, advocated caution. He was afraid he might get his brother in trouble. If they waited till some of the bottles were opened it'd be all right to take one, and everybody'd think it was one of the college fellas.

While they were still engaged in argument George Key

hurried through the room and, barely grunting at them, disappeared by way of the green baize door. A minute later
they heard several corks pop, and then the sound of crack-
ling ice and splashing liquid. George was mixing the punch.

The soldiers exchanged delighted grins.

'Oh, boy!' whispered Rose.

George reappeared.

'Just keep low, boys,' he said quickly. 'I'll have your
stuff for you in five minutes.'

He disappeared through the door by which he had come.

As soon as his footsteps receded down the stairs, Rose,
after a cautious look, darted into the room of delights and
reappeared with a bottle in his hand.

'Here's what I say,' he said, as they sat radiantly digesting their first drink. 'We'll wait till he comes up, and we'll
ask him if we can't just stay here and drink what he brings
us—see. We'll tell him we haven't got any place to drink it
—see. Then we can sneak in there whenever there ain't
nobody in that there room and tuck a bottle under our coats.
We'll have enough to last us a coupla days—see?'

'Sure,' agreed Rose enthusiastically. 'Oh, boy! And if
we want to we can sell it to sojers any time we want to.'

They were silent for a moment thinking rosily of this idea.
Then Key reached up and unhooked the collar of his O.D.
coat.

'It's hot in here, ain't it?'

Rose agreed earnestly.

'Hot as hell.'

IV

She was still quite angry when she came out of the dressing-
room and crossed the intervening parlour of politeness that
opened onto the hall—angry not so much at the actual
happening which was, after all, the merest commonplace
of her social existence, but because it had occurred on this
particular night. She had no quarrel with herself. She had
acted with that correct mixture of dignity and reticent pity

which she always employed. She had succinctly and deftly snubbed him.

It had happened when their taxi was leaving the Biltmore —hadn't gone half a block. He had lifted his right arm awkwardly—she was on his right side—and attempted to settle it snugly around the crimson fur-trimmed opera cloak she wore. This in itself had been a mistake. It was inevitably more graceful for a young man attempting to embrace a young lady of whose acquiescence he was not certain, to first put his far arm around her. It avoided that awkward movement of raising the near arm.

His second *faux pas* was unconscious. She had spent the afternoon at the hairdresser's; the idea of any calamity overtaking her hair was extremely repugnant—yet as Peter made his unfortunate attempt the point of his elbow had just faintly brushed it. That was his second *faux pas*. Two were quite enough.

He had begun to murmur. At the first murmur she had decided that he was nothing but a college boy—Edith was twenty-two, and anyhow, this dance, first of its kind since the war, was reminding her, with the accelerating rhythm of its associations, of something else—of another dance and another man, a man for whom her feelings had been little more than a sad-eyed, adolescent mooniness. Edith Bradin was falling in love with her recollection of Gordon Sterrett.

So she came out of the dressing-room at Delmonico's and stood for a second in the doorway looking over the shoulders of a black dress in front of her at the groups of Yale men who flitted like dignified black moths around the head of the stairs. From the room she had left drifted out the heavy fragrance left by the passage to and fro of many scented young beauties—rich perfumes and the fragile memory-laden dust of fragrant powders. This odour drifting out acquired the tang of cigarette smoke in the hall, and then settled sensuously down the stairs and permeated the ballroom where the Gamma Psi dance was to be held. It was an odour she knew well, exciting, stimulating, restlessly sweet—the odour of a fashionable dance.

She thought of her own appearance. Her bare arms and shoulders were powdered to a creamy white. She knew they looked very soft and would gleam like milk against the black backs that were to silhouette them to-night. The hairdressing had been a success; her reddish mass of hair was piled and crushed and creased to an arrogant marvel of mobile curves. Her lips were finely made of deep carmine; the irises of her eyes were delicate, breakable blue, like china eyes. She was a complete, infinitely delicate, quite perfect thing of beauty, flowing in an even line from a complex coiffure to two small slim feet.

She thought of what she would say to-night at this revel, faintly presaged already by the sounds of high and low laughter and slippered footsteps, and movements of couples up and down the stairs. She would talk the language she had talked for many years—her line—made up of the current expressions, bits of journalese and college slang strung together into an intrinsic whole, careless, faintly provocative, delicately sentimental. She smiled faintly as she heard a girl sitting on the stairs near her say: 'You don't know the half of it, dearie!'

And as she smiled her anger melted for a moment, and closing her eyes she drew in a deep breath of pleasure. She dropped her arms to her sides until they were faintly touching the sleek sheath that covered and suggested her figure. She had never felt her own softness so much nor so enjoyed the whiteness of her own arms.

'I smell sweet,' she said to herself simply, and then came another thought—'I'm made for love.'

She liked the sound of this and thought it again; then in inevitable succession came her new-born riot of dreams about Gordon. The twist of her imagination which, two months before, had disclosed to her her unguessed desire to see him again, seemed now to have been leading up to this dance, this hour.

For all her sleek beauty, Edith was a grave, slow-thinking girl. There was a streak in her of that same desire to ponder, of that adolescent idealism that had turned her brother socialist and pacifist. Henry Bradin had left Cornell, where he had been an instructor in economics, and had come to New York to pour the latest cures for incurable evils into the columns of a radical weekly newspaper.

Edith, less fatuously, would have been content to cure Gordon Sterrett. There was a quality of weakness in Gordon that she wanted to take care of; there was a helplessness in him that she wanted to protect. And she wanted someone she had known a long while, someone who had loved her a long while. She was a little tired; she wanted to get married. Out of a pile of letters, half a dozen pictures and as many memories, and this weariness, she had decided that next time she saw Gordon their relations were going to be changed. She would say something that would change them. There was this evening. This was her evening. All evenings were her evenings.

Then her thoughts were interrupted by a solemn under-graduate with a hurt look and an air of strained formality who presented himself before her and bowed unusually low. It was the man she had come with, Peter Himmel. He was tall and humorous, with horned-rimmed glasses and an air of attractive whimsicality. She suddenly rather disliked him—probably because he had not succeeded in kissing her.

'Well,' she began, 'are you still furious at me?'

'Not at all.'

She stepped forward and took his arm.

'I'm sorry,' she said softly. 'I don't know why I snapped out that way. I'm in a bum humour to-night for some strange reason. I'm sorry.'

'S'all right,' he mumbled, 'don't mention it.'

He felt disagreeably embarrassed. Was she rubbing in the fact of his late failure?

'It was a mistake,' she continued, on the same consciously gentle key. 'We'll both forget it.' For this he hated her.

A few minutes later they drifted out on the floor while the dozen swaying, sighing members of the specially hired jazz orchestra informed the crowded ballroom that 'if a

saxophone and me are left alone why then two is com-
pan-ee!'

A man with a moustache cut in.

'Hello,' he began reprovingly. 'You don't remember me.'

'I can't just think of your name,' she said lightly—'and
I know you so well.'

'I met you up at—' His voice trailed disconsolately off
as a man with very fair hair cut in. Edith murmured a
conventional 'Thanks, loads—cut in later,' to the *inconnu*.

The very fair man insisted on shaking hands enthusiastically. She placed him as one of the numerous Jims
of her acquaintance—last name a mystery. She remembered
even that he had a peculiar rhythm in dancing and found
as they started that she was right.

'Going to be here long?' he breathed confidentially.

She leaned back and looked up at him.

'Couple of weeks.'

'Where are you?'

'Biltmore. Call me up some day.'

'I mean it,' he assured her. 'I will. We'll go to tea.'

'So do I—Do.'

A dark man cut in with intense formality.

'You don't remember me, do you?' he said gravely.

'I should say I do. Your name's Harlan.'

'No-ope. Barlow.'

'Well, I knew there were two syllables anyway. You're
the boy that played the ukulele so well up at Howard
Marshall's house party.'

'I played—but not——'

A man with prominent teeth cut in. Edith inhaled a slight
cloud of whiskey. She liked men to have had something to
drink; they were so much more cheerful, and appreciative
and complimentary—much easier to talk to.

'My name's Dean, Philip Dean,' he said cheerfully. 'You
don't remember me, I know, but you used to come up to
New Haven with a fellow I roomed with senior year,
Gordon Sterrett.'

Edith looked up quickly.

'Yes, I went up with him twice—to the Pump and Slipper and the Junior prom.'

'You've seen him, of course,' said Dean carelessly. 'He's here to-night. I saw him just a minute ago.'

Edith started. Yet she had felt quite sure he would be here.

'Why, no, I haven't——'

A fat man with red hair cut in.

'Hello, Edith,' he began.

'Why—hello there——'

She slipped, stumbled lightly.

'I'm sorry, dear,' she murmured mechanically.

She had seen Gordon—Gordon very white and listless, leaning against the side of a doorway, smoking and looking into the ballroom. Edith could see that his face was thin and wan—that the hand he raised to his lips with a cigarette was trembling. They were dancing quite close to him now.

'—They invite so darn many extra fellas that you—' the short man was saying.

'Hello, Gordon,' called Edith over her partner's shoulder. Her heart was pounding wildly.

His large dark eyes were fixed on her. He took a step in her direction. Her partner turned her away—she heard his voice bleating——

'—but half the stags get lit and leave before long, so——'

Then a low tone at her side.

'May I, please?'

She was dancing suddenly with Gordon; one of his arms was around her; she felt it tighten spasmodically; felt his hand on her back with the fingers spread. Her hand holding the little lace handkerchief was crushed in his.

'Why Gordon,' she began breathlessly.

'Hello, Edith.'

She slipped again—was tossed forward by her recovery until her face touched the black cloth of his dinner coat. She loved him—she knew she loved him—then for a minute there was silence while a strange feeling of uneasiness crept over her. Something was wrong.

Of a sudden her heart wrenched, and turned over as she realized what it was. He was pitiful and wretched, a little drunk, and miserably tired.

'Oh—' she cried involuntarily.

His eyes looked down at her. She saw suddenly that they were blood-streaked and rolling uncontrollably.

'Gordon,' she murmured, 'we'll sit down, I want to sit down.'

They were nearly in mid-floor, but she had seen two men start toward her from opposite sides of the room, so she halted, seized Gordon's limp hand and led him bumping through the crowd, her mouth tight shut, her face a little pale under her rouge, her eyes trembling with tears.

She found a place high up on the soft-carpeted stairs, and he sat down heavily beside her.

'Well,' he began, staring at her unsteadily, 'I certainly am glad to see you, Edith.'

She looked at him without answering. The effect of this on her was immeasurable. For years she had seen men in various stages of intoxication, from uncles all the way down to chauffeurs, and her feelings had varied from amusement to disgust, but here for the first time she was seized with a new feeling—an unutterable horror.

'Gordon,' she said accusingly and almost crying, 'you look like the devil.'

He nodded. 'I've had trouble, Edith.'

'Trouble?'

'All sorts of trouble. Don't you say anything to the family, but I'm all gone to pieces. I'm a mess, Edith.'

His lower lip was sagging. He seemed scarcely to see her.

'Can't you—can't you,' she hesitated, 'can't you tell me about it, Gordon? You know I'm always interested in you.'

She bit her lip—she had intended to say something stronger, but found at the end that she couldn't bring it out.

Gordon shook his head dully. 'I can't tell you. You're a good woman. I can't tell a good woman the story.'

'Rot,' she said, defiantly. 'I think it's a perfect insult to call any one a good woman in that way. It's a slam. You've been drinking, Gordon.'

'Thanks.' He inclined his head gravely 'Thanks for the information.'

'Why do you drink?'

'Because I'm so damn miserable.'

'Do you think drinking's going to make it any better?'

'What you doing—trying to reform me?'

'No; I'm trying to help you, Gordon. Can't you tell me about it?'

'I'm in an awful mess. Best thing you can do is to pretend not to know me.'

'Why, Gordon?'

'I'm sorry I cut in on you—it's unfair to you. You're a pure woman—and all that sort of thing. Here, I'll get someone else to dance with you.'

He rose clumsily to his feet, but she reached up and pulled him down beside her on the stairs.

'Here, Gordon. You're ridiculous. You're hurting me. You're acting like a—like a crazy man——'

'I admit it. I'm a little crazy. Something's wrong with me, Edith. There's something left me. It doesn't matter.'

'It does, tell me.'

'Just that. I was always queer—little bit different from other boys. All right in college, but now it's all wrong. Things have been snapping inside me for four months like little hooks on a dress, and it's about to come off when a few more hooks go. I'm very gradually going loony.'

He turned his eyes full on her and began to laugh, and she shrank away from him.

'What *is* the matter?'

'Just me,' he repeated. 'I'm going loony. This whole place is like a dream to me—this Delmonico's——'

As he talked she saw he had changed utterly. He wasn't at all light and gay and careless—a great lethargy and discouragement had come over him. Revulsion seized her, followed by a faint, surprising boredom. His voice seemed to come out of a great void.

'Edith,' he said, 'I used to think I was clever, talented, an artist. Now I know I'm nothing. Can't draw, Edith. Don't know why I'm telling you this.'

She nodded absently.

'I can't draw, I can't do anything. I'm poor as a church mouse.' He laughed, bitterly and rather too loud. 'I've become a damn beggar, a leech on my friends. I'm a failure. I'm poor as hell.'

Her distaste was growing. She barely nodded this time, waiting for her first possible cue to rise.

Suddenly Gordon's eyes filled with tears.

'Edith,' he said, turning to her with what was evidently a strong effort at self-control, 'I can't tell you what it means to me to know there's one person left who's interested in me.'

He reached out and patted her hand, and involuntarily she drew it away.

'It's mighty fine of you,' he repeated.

'Well,' she said slowly, looking him in the eye, 'anyone's always glad to see an old friend—but I'm sorry to see you like this, Gordon.'

There was a pause while they looked at each other, and the momentary eagerness in his eyes wavered. She rose and stood looking at him, her face quite expressionless.

'Shall we dance?' she suggested, coolly.

—Love is fragile—she was thinking—but perhaps the pieces are saved, the things that hovered on lips, that might have been said. The new love words, the tenderness learned, are treasured up for the next lover.

V

Peter Himmel, escort to the lovely Edith, was unaccustomed to being snubbed; having been snubbed, he was hurt and embarrassed, and ashamed of himself. For a matter of two months he had been on special delivery terms with Edith Bradin and knowing that the one excuse and explanation of the special delivery letter is its value in sentimental correspondence, he had believed himself quite sure of his ground. He searched in vain for any reason why she should have taken this attitude in the matter of a simple kiss.

Therefore when he was cut in on by the man with the moustache he went out into the hall and, making up a sentence, said it over to himself several times. Considerably deleted, this was it:

'Well, if any girl ever led a man on and then jolted him, she did—and she has no kick coming if I go out and get beautifully boiled.'

So he walked through the supper room into a small room adjoining it, which he had located earlier in the evening. It was a room in which there were several large bowls of punch flanked by many bottles. He took a seat beside the table which held the bottles.

At the second highball, boredom, disgust, the monotony of time, the turbidity of events, sank into a vague background before which glittering cobwebs formed. Things became reconciled to themselves, things lay quietly on their shelves; the troubles of the day arranged themselves in trim formation and at his curt wish of dismissal, marched off and disappeared. And with the departure of worry came brilliant, permeating symbolism. Edith became a flighty, negligible girl, not to be worried over; rather to be laughed at. She fitted like a figure of his own dream into the surface world forming about him. He himself became in a measure symbolic, a type of the continent bacchanal, the brilliant dreamer at play.

Then the symbolic mood faded and as he sipped his third highball his imagination yielded to the warm glow and he lapsed into a state similar to floating on his back in pleasant water. It was at this point that he noticed that a green baize door near him was open about two inches, and that through the aperture a pair of eyes were watching him intently.

'Hm,' murmured Peter calmly.

The green door closed—and then opened again—a bare half inch this time.

'Peek-a-boo,' murmured Peter.

6*

The door remained stationary and then he became aware of a series of tense intermittent whispers.

'One guy.'

'What's he doin'?'

'He's sittin' lookin'.'

'He better beat it off. We gotta get another li'l' bottle.'

Peter listened while the words filtered into his consciousness.

'Now this,' he thought, 'is most remarkable.'

He was excited. He was jubilant. He felt that he had stumbled upon a mystery. Affecting an elaborate carelessness he arose and walked around the table—then, turning quickly, pulled open the green door, precipitating Private Rose into the room.

Peter bowed.

'How do you do?' he said.

Private Rose set one foot slightly in front of the other, poised for fight, flight, or compromise.

'How do you do?' repeated Peter politely.

'I'm o'right.'

'Can I offer you a drink?'

Private Rose looked at him searchingly, suspecting possible sarcasm.

'O'right,' he said finally.

Peter indicated a chair.

'Sit down.'

'I got a friend,' said Rose, 'I got a friend in there.' He pointed to the green door.

'By all means let's have him in.'

Peter crossed over, opened the door and welcomed in Private Key, very suspicious and uncertain and guilty. Chairs were found and the three took their seats around the punch bowl. Peter gave them each a highball and offered them a cigarette from his case. They accepted both with some diffidence.

'Now,' continued Peter easily, 'may I ask why you gentlemen prefer to lounge away your leisure hours in a room which is chiefly furnished, as far as I can see, with

scrubbing brushes. And when the human race has pro-
gressed to the stage where seventeen thousand chairs are
manufactured on every day except Sunday—' he paused.
Rose and Key regarded him vacantly. 'Will you tell me,'
went on Peter, 'why you choose to rest yourselves on articles
intended for the transportation of water from one place to
another?'

At this point Rose contributed a grunt to the conversation.

'And lastly,' finished Peter, 'will you tell me why, when
you are in a building beautifully hung with enormous
candelabra, you prefer to spend these evening hours under
one anaemic electric light?'

Rose looked at Key; Key looked at Rose. They laughed;
they laughed uproariously; they found it was impossible
to look at each other without laughing. But they were not
laughing with this man—they were laughing at him. To
them a man who talked after this fashion was either raving
drunk or raving crazy.

'You are Yale men, I presume,' said Peter, finishing his
highball and preparing another.

They laughed again.

'Na-ah.'

'So? I thought perhaps you might be members of that
lowly section of the university known as the Sheffield
Scientific School.'

'Na-ah.'

'Hm. Well, that's too bad. No doubt you are Harvard
men, anxious to preserve your incognito in this—this
paradise of violet blue, as the newspapers say.'

'Na-ah,' said Key scornfully, 'we was just waitin' for
somebody.'

'Ah,' exclaimed Peter, rising and filling their glasses,
'very interestin'. Had a date with a scrublady, eh?'

They both denied this indignantly.

'It's all right,' Peter reassured them, 'don't apologize. A
scrublady's as good as any lady in the world. Kipling says
"Any lady and Judy O'Grady under the skin."'

'Sure,' said Key, winking broadly at Rose.

'My case, for instance,' continued Peter, finishing his glass. 'I got a girl up there that's spoiled. Spoildest darn girl I ever saw. Refused to kiss me; no reason whatsoever. Led me on deliberately to think sure I want to kiss you and then plunk! Threw me over! What's the younger generation comin' to?'

'Say tha's hard luck,' said Key—'that's awful hard luck.'

'Oh boy!' said Rose.

'Have another?' said Peter.

'We got in a sort of fight for a while,' said Key after a pause, 'but it was too far away.'

'A fight?—tha's stuff!' said Peter, seating himself unsteadily. 'Fight 'em all! I was in the army.'

'This was a Bolshevik fella.'

'Tha's stuff!' exclaimed Peter, enthusiastic. 'That's what I say! Kill the Bolshevik! Exterminate 'em!'

'We're Americuns,' said Rose, implying a sturdy, defiant patriotism.

'Sure,' said Peter. 'Greatest race in the world! We're all Americuns! Have another.'

They had another.

VI

At one o'clock a special orchestra, special even in a day of special orchestras, arrived at Delmonico's, and its members, seating themselves arrogantly around the piano, took up the burden of providing music for the Gamma Psi Fraternity. They were headed by a famous flute-player, distinguished throughout New York for his feat of standing on his head and shimmying with his shoulders while he played the latest jazz on his flute. During his performance the lights were extinguished except for the spotlight on the flute-player and another roving beam that threw flickering shadows and changing kaleidoscopic colours over the massed dancers.

Edith had danced herself into that tired, dreamy state habitual only with débutantes, a state equivalent to the glow of a noble soul after several long highballs. Her mind floated vaguely on the bosom of her music; her partners

changed with the unreality of phantoms under the colourful
shifting dusk, and to her present coma it seemed as if days
had passed since the dance began. She had talked on many
fragmentary subjects with many men. She had been kissed
once and made love to six times. Earlier in the evening
different undergraduates had danced with her, but now,
like all the more popular girls there, she had her own
entourage—that is, half a dozen gallants had singled her
out or were alternating her charms with those of some other
chosen beauty; they cut in on her in regular, inevitable
succession.

Several times she had seen Gordon—he had been sitting
a long time on the stairway with his palm to his head, his
dull eyes fixed at an infinite speck on the floor before him,
very depressed, he looked, and quite drunk—but Edith
each time had averted her glance, hurriedly. All that seemed
long ago; her mind was passive now, her senses were lulled
to trance-like sleep; only her feet danced and her voice
talked on in hazy sentimental banter.

But Edith was not nearly so tired as to be incapable of
moral indignation when Peter Himmel cut in on her, sub-
limely and happily drunk. She gasped and looked up at him.

'Why, *Peter* !'

'I'm a li'l' stewed, Edith.'

'Why, Peter, you're a *peach*, you are! Don't you think
it's a bum way of doing—when you're with me?'

Then she smiled unwillingly, for he was looking at her
with owlish sentimentality varied with a silly spasmodic
smile.

'Darlin' Edith,' he began earnestly, 'you know I love
you, don't you?'

'You tell it well.'

'I love you—and I merely wanted you to kiss me,' he
added sadly.

His embarrassment, his shame, were both gone. She
was a mos' beautiful girl in whole worl'. Mos' beautiful
eyes, like stars above. He wanted to 'pologize—firs', for
presuming to try to kiss her; second, for drinking—but he'd

been so discouraged 'cause he had thought she was mad at him——

The red-fat man cut in, and looking up at Edith smiled radiantly.

'Did you bring any one?' she asked.

No. The red-fat man was a stag.

'Well, would you mind—would it be an awful bother for you to—to take me home to-night?' (this extreme diffidence was a charming affectation on Edith's part—she knew that the red-fat man would immediately dissolve into a paroxysm of delight).

'Bother? Why, good Lord, I'd be darn glad to! You know I'd be darn glad to.'

'Thanks *loads*! You're awfully sweet.'

She glanced at her wrist-watch. It was half-past one. And, as she said 'half-past one' to herself, it floated vaguely into her mind that her brother had told her at luncheon that he worked in the office of his newspaper until after one-thirty every evening.

Edith turned suddenly to her current partner.

'What street is Delmonico's on, anyway?'

'Street? Oh, why Fifth Avenue, of course.'

'I mean, what cross street?'

'Why—let's see—it's on Forty-fourth Street.'

This verified what she had thought. Henry's office must be across the street and just around the corner, and it occurred to her immediately that she might slip over for a moment and surprise him, float in on him, a shimmering marvel in her new crimson opera cloak and 'cheer him up.' It was exactly the sort of thing Edith revelled in doing—an unconventional, jaunty thing. The idea reached out and gripped at her imagination—after an instant's hesitation she had decided.

'My hair is just about to tumble entirely down,' she said pleasantly to her partner; 'would you mind if I go and fix it?'

'Not at all.'

'You're a peach.'

A few minutes later, wrapped in her crimson opera cloak, she flitted down a side-stairs, her cheeks glowing with excitement at her little adventure. She ran by a couple who stood at the door—a weak-chinned waiter and an over-rouged young lady, in hot dispute—and opening the outer door stepped into the warm May night.

VII

The over-rouged young lady followed her with a brief, bitter glance—then turned again to the weak-chinned waiter and took up her argument.

'You better go up and tell him I'm here,' she said defiantly, 'or I'll go up myself.'

'No, you don't!' said George sternly.

The girl smiled sardonically.

'Oh, I don't, don't I? Well, let me tell you I know more college fellas and more of 'em know me, and are glad to take me out on a party, than you ever saw in your whole life.'

'Maybe so——'

'Maybe so,' she interrupted. 'Oh, it's all right for any of 'em like that one that just ran out—God knows where *she* went—it's all right for them that are asked here to come or go as they like—but when I want to see a friend they have some cheap, ham-slinging, bring-me-a-doughnut waiter to stand here and keep me out.'

'See here,' said the elder Key indignantly, 'I can't lose my job. Maybe this fella you're talking about doesn't want to see you.'

'Oh, he wants to see me all right.'

'Anyway, how could I find him in all that crowd?'

'Oh, he'll be there,' she asserted confidently. 'You just ask anybody for Gordon Sterrett and they'll point him out to you. They all know each other, those fellas.'

She produced a mesh bag, and taking out a dollar bill handed it to George.

'Here,' she said, 'here's a bribe. You find him and give

him my message. You tell him if he isn't here in five minutes I'm coming up.'

George shook his head pessimistically, considered the question for a moment, wavered violently, and then withdrew.

In less than the allotted time Gordon came downstairs. He was drunker than he had been earlier in the evening and in a different way. The liquor seemed to have hardened on him like a crust. He was heavy and lurching—almost incoherent when he talked.

''Lo, Jewel,' he said thickly. 'Came right away. Jewel, I couldn't get that money. Tried my best.'

'Money nothing!' she snapped. 'You haven't been near me for ten days. What's the matter?'

He shook his head slowly.

'Been very low, Jewel. Been sick.'

'Why didn't you tell me if you were sick. I don't care about the money that bad. I didn't start bothering you about it at all until you began neglecting me.'

Again he shook his head.

'Haven't been neglecting you. Not at all.'

'Haven't! You haven't been near me for three weeks, unless you been so drunk you didn't know what you were doing.'

'Been sick, Jewel,' he repeated, turning his eyes upon her wearily.

'You're well enough to come and play with your society friends here all right. You told me you'd meet me for dinner, and you said you'd have some money for me. You didn't even bother to ring me up.'

'I couldn't get any money.'

'Haven't I just been saying that doesn't matter? I wanted to see *you*, Gordon, but you seem to prefer your somebody else.'

He denied this bitterly.

'Then get your hat and come along', she suggested.

Gordon hesitated—and she came suddenly close to him and slipped her arms around his neck.

'Come on with me, Gordon,' she said in a half whisper.

'We'll go over to Devineries' and have a drink, and then we can go up to my apartment.'

'I can't, Jewel,——'

'You can,' she said intensely.

'I'm sick as a dog!'

'Well, then, you oughtn't to stay here and dance.'

With a glance around him in which relief and despair were mingled, Gordon hesitated; then she suddenly pulled him to her and kissed him with soft, pulpy lips.

'All right,' he said heavily. 'I'll get my hat.'

VIII

When Edith came out into the clear blue of the May night she found the Avenue deserted. The windows of the big shops were dark; over their doors were drawn great iron masks until they were only shadowy tombs of the late day's splendour. Glancing down towards Forty-second Street she saw a commingled blur of lights from the all-night restaurants. Over on Sixth Avenue the elevated, a flare of fire, roared across the street between the glimmering parallels of light at the station and streaked along into the crisp dark. But at Forty-fourth Street it was very quiet.

Pulling her cloak close about her Edith darted across the Avenue. She started nervously as a solitary man passed her and said in a hoarse whisper—'Where bound, kiddo?' She was reminded of a night in her childhood when she had walked around the block in her pyjamas and a dog had howled at her from a mystery-big back yard.

In a minute she had reached her destination, a two-storey, comparatively old building on Forty-fourth, in the upper windows of which she thankfully detected a wisp of light. It was bright enough outside for her to make out the sign beside the window—the *New York Trumpet*. She stepped inside a dark hall and after a second saw the stairs in the corner.

Then she was in a long, low room furnished with many desks and hung on all sides with file copies of newspapers.

There were only two occupants. They were sitting at different ends of the room, each wearing a green eye-shade and writing by a solitary desk light.

For a moment she stood uncertainly in the doorway, and then both men turned around simultaneously and she recognized her brother.

'Why, Edith!' He rose quickly and approached her in surprise, removing his eye-shade. He was tall, lean, and dark, with black, piercing eyes under very thick glasses. They were far-away eyes that seemed always fixed just over the head of the person to whom he was talking.

He put his hands on her arms and kissed her cheek.

'What is it?' he repeated in some alarm.

'I was at a dance across at Delmonico's, Henry,' she said excitedly, 'and I couldn't resist tearing over to see you.'

'I'm glad you did.' His alertness gave way quickly to a habitual vagueness. 'You oughtn't to be out alone at night though, ought you?'

The man at the other end of the room had been looking at them curiously, but at Henry's beckoning gesture he approached. He was loosely fat with little twinkling eyes, and, having removed his collar and tie, he gave the impression of a Middle-Western farmer on a Sunday afternoon.

'This is my sister,' said Henry. 'She dropped in to see me.'

'How do you do?' said the fat man, smiling. 'My name's Bartholomew, Miss Bradin. I know your brother has forgotten it long ago.'

Edith laughed politely.

'Well,' he continued, 'not exactly gorgeous quarters we have here, are they?'

Edith looked around the room.

'They seem very nice,' she replied. 'Where do you keep the bombs?'

'The bombs?' repeated Bartholomew, laughing. 'That's pretty good—the bombs. Did you hear her, Henry? She wants to know where we keep the bombs. Say, that's pretty good.'

Edith swung herself around onto a vacant desk and sat

dangling her feet over the edge. Her brother took a seat beside her.

'Well,' he asked, absentmindedly, 'how do you like New York this trip?'

'Not bad. I'll be over at the Biltmore with the Hoyts until Sunday. Can't you come to luncheon to-morrow?'

He thought a moment.

'I'm especially busy,' he objected, 'and I hate women in groups.'

'All right,' she agreed, unruffled. 'Let's you and me have luncheon together.'

'Very well.'

'I'll call for you at twelve.'

Bartholomew was obviously anxious to return to his desk, but apparently considered that it would be rude to leave without some parting pleasantry.

'Well'—he began awkwardly.

They both turned to him.

'Well, we—we had an exciting time earlier in the evening.'

The two men exchanged glances.

'You should have come earlier,' continued Bartholomew, somewhat encouraged. 'We had a regular vaudeville.'

'Did you really?'

'A serenade,' said Henry. 'A lot of soldiers gathered down there in the street and began to yell at the sign.'

'Why?' she demanded.

'Just a crowd,' said Henry, abstractedly. 'All crowds have to howl. They didn't have anybody with much initiative in the lead, or they'd probably have forced their way in here and smashed things up.'

'Yes,' said Bartholomew, turning again to Edith, 'you should have been here.'

He seemed to consider this a sufficient cue for withdrawal, for he turned abruptly and went back to his desk.

'Are the soldiers all set against the Socialists?' demanded Edith of her brother. 'I mean do they attack you violently and all that?'

Henry replaced his eye-shade and yawned.

'The human race has come a long way,' he said casually, 'but most of us are throw-backs; the soldiers don't know what they want, or what they hate, or what they like. They're used to acting in large bodies, and they seem to have to make demonstrations. So it happens to be against us. There've been riots all over the city to-night. It's May Day, you see.'

'Was the disturbance here pretty serious?'

'Not a bit,' he said scornfully. 'About twenty-five of them stopped in the street about nine o'clock, and began to bellow at the moon.'

'Oh'—She changed the subject. 'You're glad to see me, Henry?'

'Why, sure.'

'You don't seem to be.'

'I am.'

'I suppose you think I'm a—a waster. Sort of the World's Worst Butterfly.'

Henry laughed.

'Not at all. Have a good time while you're young. Why? Do I seem like the priggish and earnest youth?'

'No—' She paused, '—but somehow I began thinking how absolutely different the party I'm on is from—from all your purposes. It seems sort of—of incongruous, doesn't it?—me being at a party like that, and you over here working for a thing that'll make that sort of party impossible ever any more, if your ideas work.'

'I don't think of it that way. You're young, and you're acting just as you were brought up to act. Go ahead—have a good time.'

Her feet, which had been idly swinging, stopped and her voice dropped a note.

'I wish you'd—you'd come back to Harrisburg and have a good time. Do you feel sure that you're on the right track——'

'You're wearing beautiful stockings,' he interrupted. 'What on earth are they?'

'They're embroidered,' she replied, glancing down.

'Aren't they cunning?' She raised her skirts and uncovered slim, silk-sheathed calves. 'Or do you disapprove of silk stockings?'

He seemed slightly exasperated, bent his dark eyes on her piercingly.

'Are you trying to make me out as criticizing you in any way, Edith?'

'Not at all—'

She paused. Bartholomew had uttered a grunt. She turned and saw that he had left his desk and was standing at the window.

'What is it?' demanded Henry.

'People,' said Bartholomew, and then after an instant: 'Whole jam of them. They're coming from Sixth Avenue.'

'People.'

The fat man pressed his nose to the pane.

'Soldiers, by God!' he said emphatically. 'I had an idea they'd come back.'

Edith jumped to her feet, and running over joined Bartholomew at the window.

'There's a lot of them!' she cried excitedly. 'Come here, Henry!'

Henry readjusted his shade, but kept his seat.

'Hadn't we better turn out the lights?' suggested Bartholomew.

'No. They'll go away in a minute.'

'They're not,' said Edith, peering from the window. 'They're not even thinking of going away. There's more of them coming. Look—there's a whole crowd turning the corner of Sixth Avenue.'

By the yellow glow and blue shadows of the street lamp she could see that the sidewalk was crowded with men. They were mostly in uniform, some sober, some enthusiastically drunk, and over the whole swept an incoherent clamour and shouting.

Henry rose, and going to the window exposed himself as a long silhouette against the office lights. Immediately the shouting became a steady yell, and a rattling fusillade of small missiles, corners of tobacco plugs, cigarette-boxes, and even pennies beat against the window. The sounds of the racket now began floating up the stairs as the folding doors revolved.

'They're coming up!' cried Bartholomew.

Edith turned anxiously to Henry.

'They're coming up, Henry.'

From downstairs in the lower hall their cries were now quite audible.

'—God damn Socialists!'

'Pro-Germans! Boche-lovers!'

'Second floor, front! Come on.'

'We'll get the sons——'

The next five minutes passed in a dream. Edith was conscious that the clamour burst suddenly upon the three of them like a cloud of rain, that there was a thunder of many feet on the stairs, that Henry had seized her arm and drawn her back towards the rear of the office. Then the door opened and an overflow of men were forced into the room—not the leaders, but simply those who happened to be in front.

'Hello, Bo!'

'Up late, ain't you?'

'You an' your girl. Damn *you*!'

She noticed that two very drunken soldiers had been forced to the front, where they wobbled fatuously—one of them was short and dark, the other was tall and weak of chin.

Henry stepped forward and raised his hand.

'Friends!' he said.

The clamour faded into a momentary stillness, punctuated with mutterings.

'Friends!' he repeated, his far-away eyes fixed over the heads of the crowd, 'you're injuring no one but yourselves by breaking in here to-night. Do we look like rich men? Do we look like Germans? I ask you in all fairness——'

'Pipe down!'

'I'll say you do!'

'Say, who's your lady friend, buddy?'

A man in civilian clothes, who had been pawing over a table, suddenly held up a newspaper.

'Here it is!' he shouted. 'They wanted the Germans to win the war!'

A new overflow from the stairs was shouldered in and of a sudden the room was full of men all closing around the pale little group at the back. Edith saw that the tall soldier with the weak chin was still in front. The short dark one had disappeared.

She edged slightly backward, stood close to the open window, through which came a clear breath of cool night air.

Then the room was a riot. She realized that the soldiers were surging forward, glimpsed the fat man swinging a chair over his head—instantly the lights went out, and she felt the push of warm bodies under rough cloth, and her ears were full of shouting and trampling and hard breathing.

A figure flashed by her out of nowhere, tottered, was edged sideways, and of a sudden disappeared helplessly out through the open window with a frightened, fragmentary cry that died staccato on the bosom of the clamour. By the faint light streaming from the building backing on the area Edith had a quick impression that it had been the tall soldier with the weak chin.

Anger rose astonishingly in her. She swung her arms wildly, edged blindly towards the thickest of the scuffling. She heard grunts, curses, the muffled impact of fists.

'Henry!' she called frantically, 'Henry!'

Then, it was minutes later, she felt suddenly that there were other figures in the room. She heard a voice, deep, bullying, authoritative; she saw yellow rays of light sweeping here and there in the fracas. The cries became more scattered. The scuffling increased and then stopped.

Suddenly the lights were on and the room was full of policemen, clubbing left and right. The deep voice boomed out:

'Here now! Here now! Here now!'

And then:

'Quiet down and get out! Here now!'

The room seemed to empty like a wash-bowl. A police-man fast-grappled in the corner released his hold on his soldier antagonist and started him with a shove towards the door. The deep voice continued. Edith perceived now that it came from a bull-necked police captain standing near the door.

'Here now! This is no way! One of your own sojers got shoved out of the back window an' killed hisself!'

'Henry!' called Edith, 'Henry!'

She beat wildly with her fists on the back of the man in front of her; she brushed between two others; fought, shrieked, and beat her way to a very pale figure sitting on the floor close to a desk.

'Henry,' she cried passionately, 'what's the matter? What's the matter? Did they hurt you?'

His eyes were shut. He groaned and then looking up said disgustedly——

'They broke my leg. My God, the fools!'

'Here now!' called the police captain. 'Here now! Here now!'

IX

'Childs', Fifty-ninth Street,' at eight o'clock of any morn-ing differs from its sisters by less than the width of their marble tables or the degree of polish on the frying-pans. You will see there a crowd of poor people with sleep in the corners of their eyes, trying to look straight before them at their food so as not to see the other poor people. But Childs', Fifty-ninth, four hours earlier is quite unlike any Childs' restaurant from Portland, Oregon, to Portland, Maine. Within its pale but sanitary walls one finds a noisy medley of chorus girls, college boys, débutantes, rakes, *filles de joie* —a not unrepresentative mixture of the gayest of Broadway, and even of Fifth Avenue.

In the early morning of May the second it was unusually full. Over the marble-topped tables were bent the excited faces of flappers whose fathers owned individual villages. They were eating buckwheat cakes and scrambled eggs with relish and gusto, an accomplishment that it would have been utterly impossible for them to repeat in the same place four hours later.

Almost the entire crowd were from the Gamma Psi dance at Delmonico's except for several chorus girls from a midnight revue who sat at a side table and wished they'd taken off a little more make-up after the show. Here and there a drab, mouse-like figure, desperately out of place, watched the butterflies with a weary, puzzled curiosity. But the drab figure was the exception. This was the morning after May Day, and celebration was still in the air.

Gus Rose, sober but a little dazed, must be classed as one of the drab figures. How he had got himself from Forty-fourth Street to Fifty-ninth Street after the riot was only a hazy half-memory. He had seen the body of Carrol Key put in an ambulance and driven off, and then he had started up town with two or three soldiers. Somewhere between Forty-fourth Street and Fifty-ninth Street the other soldiers had met some women and disappeared. Rose had wandered to Columbus Circle and chosen the gleaming lights of Childs' to minister to his craving for coffee and doughnuts. He walked in and sat down.

All around him floated airy, inconsequential chatter and high-pitched laughter. At first he failed to understand, but after a puzzled five minutes he realized that this was the aftermath of some gay party. Here and there a restless, hilarious young man wandered fraternally and familiarly between the tables, shaking hands indiscriminately and pausing occasionally for a facetious chat, while excited waiters, bearing cakes and eggs aloft, swore at him silently, and bumped him out of the way. To Rose, seated at the most inconspicuous and least crowded table, the whole scene was a colourful circus of beauty and riotous pleasure.

He became gradually aware, after a few moments, that the couple seated diagonally across from him, with their backs to the crowd, were not the least interesting pair in the room. The man was drunk. He wore a dinner coat with a dishevelled tie and shirt swollen by spillings of water and wine. His eyes, dim and bloodshot, roved unnaturally from side to side. His breath came short between his lips.

'He's been on a spree!' thought Rose.

The woman was almost if not quite sober. She was pretty, with dark eyes and feverish high colour, and she kept her active eyes fixed on her companion with the alertness of a hawk. From time to time she would lean and whisper intently to him, and he would answer by inclining his head heavily or by a particularly ghoulish and repellent wink.

Rose scrutinized them dumbly for some minutes, until the woman gave him a quick, resentful look; then he shifted his gaze to two of the most conspicuously hilarious of the promenaders who were on a protracted circuit of the tables. To his surprise he recognized in one of them the young man by whom he had been so ludicrously entertained at Delmonico's. This started him thinking of Key with a vague sentimentality, not unmixed with awe. Key was dead. He had fallen thirty-five feet and split his skull like a cracked coconut.

'He was a darn good guy,' thought Rose mournfully. 'He was a darn good guy, o'right. That was awful hard luck about him.'

The two promenaders approached and started down between Rose's table and the next, addressing friends and strangers alike with jovial familiarity. Suddenly Rose saw the fair-haired one with the prominent teeth stop, look unsteadily at the man and girl opposite, and then begin to move his head disapprovingly from side to side.

The man with the blood-shot eyes looked up.

'Gordy,' said the promenader with the prominent teeth, 'Gordy.'

'Hello,' said the man with the stained shirt thickly.

Prominent Teeth shook his finger pessimistically at the pair, giving the woman a glance of aloof condemnation.

'What'd I tell you Gordy?'

Gordon stirred in his seat.

'Go to hell!' he said.

Dean continued to stand there shaking his finger. The woman began to get angry.

'You go away!' she cried fiercely. 'You're drunk, that's what you are!'

'So's he,' suggested Dean, staying the motion of his finger and pointing it at Gordon.

Peter Himmel ambled up, owlish now and oratorically inclined.

'Here now,' he began, as if called upon to deal with some petty dispute between children. 'Wha's all trouble?'

'You take your friend away,' said Jewel tartly. 'He's bothering us.'

'What's 'at?'

'You heard me!' she said shrilly. 'I said to take your drunken friend away.'

Her rising voice rang out above the clatter of the restaurant and a waiter came hurrying up.

'You gotta be more quiet!'

'That fella's drunk,' she cried. 'He's insulting us.'

'Ah-ha, Gordy,' persisted the accused. 'What'd I tell you.' He turned to the waiter. 'Gordy an' I friends. Been tryin' help him, haven't I, Gordy?'

Gordy looked up.

'Help me? Hell, no!'

Jewel rose suddenly, and seizing Gordon's arm assisted him to his feet.

'Come on, Gordy!' she said, leaning towards him and speaking in a half whisper. 'Let's get out of here. This fella's got a mean drunk on.'

Gordon allowed himself to be urged to his feet and started towards the door. Jewel turned for a second and addressed the provoker of their flight.

'I know all about you!' she said fiercely. 'Nice friend, you are, I'll say. He told me about you.'

Then she seized Gordon's arm, and together they made

their way through the curious crowd, paid their check, and
went out.

'You'll have to sit down,' said the waiter to Peter after
they had gone.

'What's 'at? Sit down?'

'Yes—or get out.'

Peter turned to Dean.

'Come on,' he suggested. 'Let's beat up this waiter.'

'All right.'

They advanced towards him, their faces grown stern.
The waiter retreated.

Peter suddenly reached over to a plate on the table beside
him and picking up a handful of hash tossed it into the air.
It descended as a languid parabola in snowflake effect on the
heads of those near by.

'Hey! Ease up!'

'Put him out!'

'Sit down, Peter!'

'Cut out that stuff!'

Peter laughed and bowed.

'Thank you for your kind applause, ladies and gents. If
someone will lend me some more hash and a tall hat we will
go on with the act.'

The bouncer hustled up.

'You've gotta get out!' he said to Peter.

'Hell, no!'

'He's my friend!' put in Dean indignantly.

A crowd of waiters were gathering. 'Put him out!'

'Better go, Peter.'

There was a short struggle and the two were edged and
pushed towards the door.

'I got a hat and a coat here!' cried Peter.

'Well, go get 'em and be spry about it!'

The bouncer released his hold on Peter, who, adopting a
ludicrous air of extreme cunning, rushed immediately
around to the other table, where he burst into derisive
laughter and thumbed his nose at the exasperated
waiters.

'Think I just better wait a l'il' longer,' he announced.

The chase began. Four waiters were sent around one way and four another. Dean caught hold of two of them by the coat, and another struggle took place before the pursuit of Peter could be resumed; he was finally pinioned after over-turning a sugar-bowl and several cups of coffee. A fresh argument ensued at the cashier's desk, where Peter attempted to buy another dish of hash to take with him and throw at policemen.

But the commotion upon his exit proper was dwarfed by another phenomenon which drew admiring glances and a prolonged involuntary ' Oh-h-h!' from every person in the restaurant.

The great plate-glass front had turned to a deep creamy blue, the colour of a Maxfield Parrish moonlight—a blue that seemed to press close upon the pane as if to crowd its way into the restaurant. Dawn had come up in Columbus Circle, magical, breathless dawn, silhouetting the great statue of the immortal Christopher, and mingling in a curious and uncanny manner with the fading yellow electric light inside.

X

Mr In and Mr Out are not listed by the census-taker. You will search for them in vain through the social register or the births, marriages, and deaths, or the grocer's credit list. Oblivion has swallowed them and the testimony that they ever existed at all is vague and shadowy, and inadmissible in a court of law. Yet I have it upon the best authority that for a brief space Mr In and Mr Out lived, breathed, answered to their names and radiated vivid personalities of their own.

During the brief span of their lives they walked in their native garments down the great highway of a great nation; were laughed at, sworn at, chased, and fled from. Then they passed and were heard of no more.

They were already taking form dimly, when a taxicab with

the top open breezed down Broadway in the faintest glim-
mer of May dawn. In this car sat the souls of Mr In and
Mr Out discussing with amazement the blue light that had
so precipitately coloured the sky behind the statue of
Christopher Columbus, discussing with bewilderment the
old, grey faces of the early risers which skimmed palely
along the street like blown bits of paper on a grey lake. They
were agreed on all things, from the absurdity of the bouncer
in Childs' to the absurdity of the business of life. They were
dizzy with the extreme maudlin happiness that the morning
had awakened in their glowing souls. Indeed, so fresh and
vigorous was their pleasure in living that they felt it should
be expressed by loud cries.

'Ye-ow-ow!' hooted Peter, making a megaphone with
his hands—and Dean joined in with a call that, though
equally significant and symbolic, derived its resonance from
its very inarticulateness.

'Yo-ho! Yea! Yoho! Yo-buba!'

Fifty-third Street was a bus with a dark, bobbed-hair
beauty atop; Fifty-second was a street cleaner who dodged,
escaped, and sent up a yell of, 'Look where you're aimin'!'
in a pained and grieved voice. At Fiftieth Street a group of
men on a very white sidewalk in front of a very white building turned to stare after them, and shouted:

'Some party, boys!'

At Forty-ninth Street Peter turned to Dean. 'Beautiful
morning,' he said gravely, squinting up his owlish eyes.

'Probably is.'

'Go get some breakfast, hey?'

Dean agreed—with additions.

'Breakfast and liquor.'

'Breakfast and liquor,' repeated Peter, and they looked
at each other, nodding. 'That's logical.'

Then they both burst into loud laughter.

'Breakfast and liquor! Oh, gosh!'

'No such thing,' announced Peter.

'Don't serve it? Ne'mind. We force 'em serve it. Bring
pressure bear.'

'Bring logic bear.'

The taxi cut suddenly off Broadway, sailed along a cross street, and stopped in front of a heavy tomb-like building in Fifth Avenue.

'What's idea?'

The taxi-driver informed them that this was Delmonico's.

This was somewhat puzzling. They were forced to devote several minutes to intense concentration, for if such an order had been given there must have been a reason for it.

'Somep'm 'bouta coat,' suggested the taxi-man.

That was it. Peter's overcoat and hat. He had left them at Delmonico's. Having decided this, they disembarked from the taxi and strolled towards the entrance arm in arm.

'Hey!' said the taxi-driver.

'Huh?'

'You better pay me.'

They shook their heads in shocked negation.

'Later, not now—we give orders, you wait.'

The taxi-driver objected; he wanted his money now. With the scornful condescension of men exercising tremendous self-control they paid him.

Inside Peter groped in vain through a dim, deserted check-room in search of his coat and derby.

'Gone, I guess. Somebody stole it.'

'Some Sheff student.'

'All probability.'

'Never mind,' said Dean, nobly. 'I'll leave mine here too —then we'll both be dressed the same.'

He removed his overcoat and hat and was hanging them up when his roving glance was caught and held magnetically by two large squares of cardboard tacked to the two coat-room doors. The one on the left-hand bore the word 'In' in big black letters, and the one on the right-hand door flaunted the equally emphatic word 'Out.'

'Look!' he exclaimed happily——

Peter's eyes followed his pointing finger.

'What?'

'Look at the signs. Let's take 'em.'

'Good idea.'

'Probably pair very rare an' valuable signs. Probably come in handy.'

Peter removed the left-hand sign from the door and endeavoured to conceal it about his person. The sign being of considerable proportions, this was a matter of some difficulty. An idea flung itself at him, and with an air of dignified mystery he turned his back. After an instant he wheeled dramatically around, and stretching out his arms displayed himself to the admiring Dean. He had inserted the sign in his vest, completely covering his shirt front. In effect, the word 'In' had been painted upon his shirt in large black letters.

'Yoho!' cheered Dean. 'Mister In.'

He inserted his own sign in like manner.

'Mister Out!' he announced triumphantly. 'Mr In meet Mr Out.'

They advanced and shook hands. Again laughter overcame them and they rocked in a shaken spasm of mirth.

'Yoho!'

'We probably get a flock of breakfast.'

'We'll go—go to the Commodore.'

Arm in arm they sallied out the door, and turning east in Forty-fourth Street set out for the Commodore.

As they came out a short dark soldier, very pale and tired, who had been wandering listlessly along the sidewalk, turned to look at them.

He started over as though to address them, but as they immediately bent on him glances of withering unrecognition, he waited until they had started unsteadily down the street, and then followed at about forty paces, chuckling to himself and saying, 'Oh, boy!' over and over under his breath, in delighted, anticipatory tones.

Mr In and Mr Out were meanwhile exchanging pleasantries concerning their future plans.

'We want liquor; we want breakfast. Neither without the other. One and indivisible.'

'We want both 'em!'

'Both 'em!'

It was quite light now, and passers-by began to bend curious eyes on the pair. Obviously they were engaged in a discussion, which afforded each of them intense amusement, for occasionally a fit of laughter would seize upon them so violently that, still with their arms interlocked, they would bend nearly double.

Reaching the Commodore, they exchanged a few spicy epigrams with the sleepy-eyed doorman, navigated the revolving door with some difficulty, and then made their way through a thinly populated but startled lobby to the dining-room, where a puzzled waiter showed them an obscure table in a corner. They studied the bill of fare helplessly, telling over the items to each other in puzzled mumbles.

'Don't see any liquor here,' said Peter reproachfully.

The waiter became audible but unintelligible.

'Repeat,' continued Peter, with patient tolerance, 'that there seems to be unexplained and quite distasteful lack of liquor upon bill of fare.'

'Here!' said Dean confidently, 'let me handle him.' He turned to the waiter—'Bring us—bring us—' he scanned the bill of fare anxiously. 'Bring us a quart of champagne and a—a—probably ham sandwich.'

The waiter looked doubtful.

'Bring it!' roared Mr In and Mr Out in chorus.

The waiter coughed and disappeared. There was a short wait during which they were subjected without their knowledge to a careful scrutiny by the head waiter. Then the champagne arrived, and at the sight of it Mr In and Mr Out became jubilant.

'Imagine their objecting to us having champagne for breakfast—jus' imagine.'

They both concentrated upon the vision of such an awesome possibility, but the feat was too much for them. It was impossible for their joint imaginations to conjure up a world where anyone might object to anyone else having

7+s.f.

champagne for breakfast. The waiter drew the cork with
an enormous *pop*—and their glasses immediately foamed
with pale yellow froth.

'Here's health, Mr In.'

'Here's the same to you, Mr Out.'

The waiter withdrew; the minutes passed; the champagne became low in the bottle.

'It's—it's mortifying,' said Dean suddenly.

'Wha's mortifying?'

'The idea their objecting us having champagne breakfast.'

'Mortifying?' Peter considered. 'Yes, tha's word—
mortifying.'

Again they collapsed into laughter, howled, swayed,
rocked back and forth in their chairs, repeating the word
'mortifying' over and over to each other—each repetition
seeming to make it only more brilliantly absurd.

After a few more gorgeous minutes they decided on
another quart. Their anxious waiter consulted his immediate superior, and this discreet person gave implicit
instructions that no more champagne should be served.
Their check was brought.

Five minutes later, arm in arm, they left the Commodore
and made their way through a curious, staring crowd along
Forty-second Street, and up Vanderbilt Avenue to the
Biltmore. There, with sudden cunning, they rose to the
occasion and traversed the lobby, walking fast and standing
unnaturally erect.

Once in the dining-room they repeated their performance. They were torn between intermittent convulsive
laughter and sudden spasmodic discussions of politics,
college, and the sunny state of their dispositions. Their
watches told them it was now nine o'clock, and a dim idea
was born in them that they were on a memorable party,
something that they would remember always. They lingered
over the second bottle. Either of them had only to mention
the word 'mortifying' to send them both into riotous gasps.
The dining-room was whirring and shifting now; a curious
lightness permeated and rarefied the heavy air.

They paid their check and walked out into the lobby.

It was at this moment that the exterior doors revolved for the thousandth time that morning, and admitted into the lobby a very pale young beauty with dark circles under her eyes, attired in a much-rumpled evening dress. She was accompanied by a plain stout man, obviously not an appropriate escort.

At the top of the stairs this couple encountered Mr In and Mr Out.

'Edith,' began Mr In, stepping towards her hilariously and making a sweeping bow, 'darling, good morning.'

The stout man glanced questioningly at Edith, as if merely asking her permission to throw this man summarily out of the way.

''Scuse familiarity,' added Peter, as an afterthought. 'Edith, good-morning.'

He seized Dean's elbow and impelled him into the foreground.

'Meet Mr Out, Edith, my bes' frien'. Inseparable. Mr In and Mr Out.'

Mr Out advanced and bowed; in fact, he advanced so far and bowed so low that he tipped slightly forward and only kept his balance by placing a hand lightly on Edith's shoulder.

'I'm Mr Out, Edith,' he mumbled pleasantly, 'S'misterin Misterout.'

''Smisterinanout,' said Peter proudly.

But Edith stared straight by them, her eyes fixed on some infinite speck in the gallery above her. She nodded slightly to the stout man, who advanced bull-like and with a sturdy brisk gesture pushed Mr In and Mr Out to either side. Through this alley he and Edith walked.

But ten paces farther on Edith stopped again—stopped and pointed to a short, dark soldier who was eyeing the crowd in general, and the tableau of Mr In and Mr Out in particular, with a sort of puzzled, spell-bound awe.

'There,' cried Edith. 'See there!'

Her voice rose, became somewhat shrill. Her pointing finger shook slightly.

'There's the soldier who broke my brother's leg.'

There were a dozen exclamations; a man in a cutaway coat left his place near the desk and advanced alertly; the stout person made a sort of lightning-like spring towards the short, dark soldier, and then the lobby closed around the little group and blotted them from the sight of Mr In and Mr Out.

But to Mr In and Mr Out this event was merely a particoloured iridescent segment of a whirring, spinning world.

They heard loud voices; they saw the stout man spring; the picture suddenly blurred.

Then they were in an elevator bound skyward.

'What floor, please?' said the elevator man.

'Any floor,' said Mr In.

'Top floor,' said Mr Out.

'This is the top floor,' said the elevator man.

'Have another floor put on,' said Mr Out.

'Higher,' said Mr In.

'Heaven,' said Mr Out.

XI

In a bedroom of a small hotel just off Sixth Avenue Gordon Sterrett awoke with a pain in the back of his head and a sick throbbing in all his veins. He looked at the dusky grey shadows in the corners of the room and at a raw place on a large leather chair in the corner where it had long been in use. He saw clothes, dishevelled, rumpled clothes on the floor and he smelt stale cigarette smoke and stale liquor. The windows were tight shut. Outside the bright sunlight had thrown a dust-filled beam across the sill—a beam broken by the head of the wide wooden bed in which he had slept. He lay very quiet—comatose, drugged, his eyes wide, his mind clicking wildly like an unoiled machine.

It must have been thirty seconds after he perceived the

sunbeam with the dust on it and the rip on the large leather chair that he had the sense of life close beside him, and it was another thirty seconds after that before he realized he was irrevocably married to Jewel Hudson.

He went out half an hour later and bought a revolver at a sporting goods store. Then he took a taxi to the room where he had been living on East Twenty-seventh Street, and, leaning across the table that held his drawing materials, fired a cartridge into his head just behind the temple.

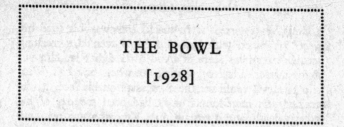

THE BOWL

[1928]

THERE was a man in my class at Princeton who never went to football games. He spent his Saturday afternoons delving for minutiae about Greek athletics and the somewhat fixed battles between Christians and wild beasts under the Antonines. Lately—several years out of college—he has discovered football players and is making etchings of them in the manner of the late George Bellows. But he was once unresponsive to the very spectacle at his door, and I suspect the originality of his judgments on what is beautiful, what is remarkable and what is fun.

I revelled in football, as audience, amateur statistician and foiled participant—for I had played in prep school, and once there was a headline in the school newspaper: 'Deering and Mullins Star Against Taft in Stiff Game Saturday.' When I came in to lunch after the battle the school stood up and clapped and the visiting coach shook hands with me and prophesied—incorrectly—that I was going to be heard from. The episode is laid away in the most pleasant lavender of my past. That year I grew very tall and thin, and when at Princeton the following fall I looked anxiously over the freshman candidates and saw the polite disregard with which they looked back at me, I realized that that particular dream was over. Keene said he might make me into a very fair pole vaulter —and he did—but it was a poor substitute; and my terrible disappointment that I wasn't going to be a great football player was probably the foundation of my friendship with Dolly Harlan. I want to begin this story about Dolly with a little rehashing of the Yale game up at New Haven, sophomore year.

Dolly was started at halfback; this was his first big game. I roomed with him and I had scented something peculiar about his state of mind, so I didn't let him out of the corner of my eye during the whole first half. With field glasses I could see the expression on his face; it was strained and incredulous, as it had been the day of his father's death, and it remained so, long after any nervousness had had time to wear off. I thought he was sick and wondered why Keene didn't see and take him out; it wasn't until later that I learned what was the matter.

It was the Yale Bowl. The size of it or the enclosed shape of it or the height of the sides had begun to get on Dolly's nerves when the team practised there the day before. In that practice he dropped one or two punts, for almost the first time in his life, and he began thinking it was because of the Bowl.

There is a new disease called agoraphobia—afraid of crowds—and another called siderodromophobia—afraid of railroad travelling—and my friend Doctor Glock, the psychoanalyst, would probably account easily for Dolly's state of mind. But here's what Dolly told me afterwards:

'Yale would punt and I'd look up. The minute I looked up, the sides of that damn pan would seem to go shooting up too. Then when the ball started to come down, the sides began leaning forward and bending over me until I could see all the people on the top seats screaming at me and shaking their fists. At the last minute I couldn't see the ball at all, but only the Bowl; every time it was just luck that I was under it and every time I juggled it in my hands.'

To go back to the game. I was in the cheering section with a good seat on the forty-yard line—good, that is, except when a very vague graduate, who had lost his friends and his hat, stood up in front of me at intervals and faltered, 'Stob Ted Coy!' under the impression that we were watching a game played a dozen years before. When he realized finally that he was funny he began performing for the gallery and aroused a chorus of whistles and boos until he was dragged unwillingly under the stand.

It was a good game—what is known in college publications as a historic game. A picture of the team that played it now hangs in every barber shop in Princeton, with Captain Gottlieb in the middle wearing a white sweater, to show that they won a championship. Yale had had a poor season, but they had the breaks in the first quarter, which ended 3 to 0 in their favour.

Between quarters I watched Dolly. He walked around panting and sucking a water bottle and still wearing that strained stunned expression. Afterwards he told me he was saying over and over to himself: 'I'll speak to Roper. I'll tell him between halves. I'll tell him I can't go through this any more.' Several times already he had felt an almost irresistible impulse to shrug his shoulders and trot off the field, for it was not only this unexpected complex about the Bowl; the truth was that Dolly fiercely and bitterly hated the game.

He hated the long, dull period of training, the element of personal conflict, the demand on his time, the monotony of the routine and the nervous apprehension of disaster just before the end. Sometimes he imagined that all the others detested it as much as he did, and fought down their aversion as he did and carried it around inside them like a cancer that they were afraid to recognize. Sometimes he imagined that a man here and there was about to tear off the mask and say, 'Dolly, do you hate this lousy business as much as I do?'

His feeling had begun back at St Regis' School and he had come up to Princeton with the idea that he was through with football for ever. But upper classmen from St Regis kept stopping him on the campus and asking him how much he weighed, and he was nominated for vice president of our class on the strength of his athletic reputation—and it was autumn, with achievement in the air. He wandered down to freshman practice one afternoon, feeling oddly lost and dissatisfied, and smelled the

turf and smelled the thrilling season. In half an hour he
was lacing on a pair of borrowed shoes and two weeks
later he was captain of the freshman team.

Once committed, he saw that he had made a mistake;
he even considered leaving college. For, with his decision
to play, Dolly assumed a moral responsibility, personal
to him, besides. To lose or to let down, or to be let
down, was simply intolerable to him. It offended his
Scotch sense of waste. Why sweat blood for an hour with
only defeat at the end?

Perhaps the worst of it was that he wasn't really a star
player. No team in the country could have spared using
him, but he could do no spectacular thing superlatively
well, neither run, pass nor kick. He was five-feet-eleven
and weighed a little more than a hundred and sixty; he
was a first-rate defensive man, sure in interference, a fair
line plunger and a fair punter. He never fumbled and
he was never inadequate; his presence, his constant cold
sure aggression, had a strong effect on other men. Morally,
he captained any team he played on and that was why
Roper had spent so much time trying to get length in his
kicks all season—he wanted him in the game.

In the second quarter Yale began to crack. It was a
mediocre team composed of flashy material, but un-
co-ordinated because of injuries and impending changes
in the Yale coaching system. The quarterback, Josh Logan,
had been a wonder at Exeter—I could testify to that—
where games can be won by the sheer confidence and spirit
of a single man. But college teams are too highly organized
to respond so simply and boyishly, and they recover less
easily from fumbles and errors of judgment behind the
line.

So, with nothing to spare, with much grunting and
straining, Princeton moved steadily down the field. On the
Yale twenty-yard line things suddenly happened. A Princeton pass was intercepted; the Yale man, excited by his own
opportunity, dropped the ball and it bobbled leisurely in
the general direction of the Yale goal. Jack Devlin and

Dolly Harlan of Princeton and somebody—I forget who—
from Yale were all about the same distance from it. What
Dolly did in that split second was all instinct; it presented
no problem to him. He was a natural athlete and in a
crisis his nervous system thought for him. He might have
raced the two others for the ball; instead, he took out the
Yale man with savage precision while Devlin scooped up
the ball and ran ten yards for a touchdown.

This was when the sports writers still saw games through
the eyes of Ralph Henry Barbour. The press box was
right behind me, and as Princeton lined up to kick goal
I heard the radio man ask:

'Who's Number 22?'

'Harlan.'

'Harlan is going to kick goal. Devlin, who made the
touchdown, comes from Lawrenceville School. He is
twenty years old. The ball went true between the bars.'

Between the halves, as Dolly sat shaking with fatigue
in the locker room, Little, the backfield coach, came and
sat beside him.

'When the ends are right on you, don't be afraid to make
a fair catch,' Little said. 'That big Havemeyer is liable to
jar the ball right out of your hands.'

Now was the time to say it: 'I wish you'd tell Bill——'
But the words twisted themselves into a trivial question
about the wind. His feeling would have to be explained,
gone into, and there wasn't time. His own self seemed
less important in this room, redolent with the tired breath,
the ultimate effort, the exhaustion of ten other men. He
was shamed by a harsh sudden quarrel that broke out
between an end and tackle; he resented the former players
in the room—especially the graduate captain of two years
before, who was a little tight and over-vehement about the
referee's favouritism. It seemed terrible to add one more
jot to all this strain and annoyance. But he might have
come out with it all the same if Little hadn't kept saying
in a low voice: 'What a take-out, Dolly! What a beautiful

take-out!' and if Little's hand hadn't rested there patting his shoulder.

II

In the third quarter Joe Dougherty kicked an easy field goal from the twenty-yard line and we felt safe, until towards twilight a series of desperate forward passes brought Yale close to a score. But Josh Logan had exhausted his personality in sheer bravado and he was outguessed by the defence at the last. As the substitutes came running in, Princeton began a last march down the field. Then abruptly it was over and the crowd poured from the stands, and Gottlieb, grabbing the ball, leaped up in the air. For a while everything was confused and crazy and happy; I saw some freshmen try to carry Dolly, but they were shy and he got away.

We all felt a great personal elation. We hadn't beaten Yale for three years and now everything was going to be all right. It meant a good winter at college, something pleasant and slick to think back upon in the damp cold days after Christmas, when a bleak futility settles over a university town. Down on the field, an improvised and uproarious team ran through plays with a derby, until the snake dance rolled over them and blotted them out. Outside the Bowl, I saw two abysmally gloomy and disgusted Yale men get into a waiting taxi and in a tone of final abnegation tell the driver 'New York.' You couldn't find Yale men; in the manner of the vanquished, they had absolutely melted away.

I begin Dolly's story with my memories of this game because that evening the girl walked into it. She was a friend of Josephine Pickman's and the four of us were going to drive up to the Midnight Frolic in New York. When I suggested to him that he'd be too tired he laughed dryly—he'd have gone anywhere that night to get the feel and rhythm of football out of his head. He walked into the hall of Josephine's house at half-past six, looking as if he'd spent the day in the barber shop save for a small and fetching strip of court plaster over one eye. He was one of the handsomest men I ever knew, anyhow; he appeared tall and slender in street clothes, his hair was dark, his eyes big and sensitive and dark, his nose aquiline and, like all his features, somehow romantic. It didn't occur to me then, but I suppose he was pretty vain—not conceited, but vain —for he always dressed in brown or soft light grey, with black ties, and people don't match themselves so successfully by accident.

He was smiling a little to himself as he came in. He shook my hand buoyantly and said, 'Why, what a surprise to meet you here, Mr Deering,' in a kidding way. Then he saw the girls through the long hall, one dark and shining, like himself, and one with gold hair that was foaming and frothing in the firelight, and said in the happiest voice I've ever heard, 'Which one is mine?'

'Either one you want, I guess.'

'Seriously, which is Pickman?'

'She's light.'

'Then the other one belongs to me. Isn't that the idea?'

'I think I'd better warn them about the state you're in.'

Miss Thorne, small, flushed and lovely, stood beside the fire. Dolly went right up to her.

'You're mine,' he said; 'you belong to me.'

She looked at him coolly, making up her mind; suddenly she liked him and smiled. But Dolly wasn't satisfied. He wanted to do something incredibly silly or startling to express his untold jubilation that he was free.

'I love you,' he said. He took her hand, his brown velvet eyes regarding her tenderly, unseeingly, convincingly. 'I love you.'

For a moment the corners of her lips fell as if in dismay that she had met someone stronger, more confident, more challenging than herself. Then, as she drew herself together visibly, he dropped her hand and the little scene in which he had expended the tension of the afternoon was over.

It was a bright cold November night and the rush of air past the open car brought a vague excitement, a sense that we were hurrying at top speed towards a brilliant destiny. The road were packed with cars that came to long inexplicable halts while police, blinded by the lights, walked up and down the line giving obscure commands. Before we had been gone an hour New York began to be a distant hazy glow against the sky.

Miss Thorne, Josephine told me, was from Washington, and had just come down from a visit in Boston.

'For the game?' I said.

'No; she didn't go to the game.'

'That's too bad. If you'd let me know I could have picked up a seat——'

'She wouldn't have gone. Vienna never goes to games.'

I remembered now that she hadn't even murmured the conventional congratulations to Dolly.

'She hates football. Her brother was killed in a prep-school game last year. I wouldn't have brought her to-night, but when we got home from the game I saw she'd been sitting there holding a book open at the same page all afternoon. You see, he was this wonderful kid and her family saw it happen and naturally never got over it.'

'But does she mind being with Dolly?'

'Of course not. She just ignores football. If anyone mentions it she simply changes the subject.'

I was glad that it was Dolly and not, say, Jack Devlin who was sitting back there with her. And I felt rather sorry for Dolly. However strongly he felt about the game, he must have waited for some acknowledgment that his effort had existed.

He was probably giving her credit for subtle consideration—yet, as the images of the afternoon flashed into his mind he might have welcomed a compliment to which he could respond 'What nonsense!' Neglected entirely, the images would become insistent and obtrusive.

I turned around and was somewhat startled to find that

Miss Thorne was in Dolly's arms; I turned quickly back and decided to let them take care of themselves.

As we waited for a traffic light on upper Broadway, I saw a sporting extra headlined with the score of the game. The green sheet was more real than the afternoon itself— succinct, condensed and clear:

PRINCETON CONQUERS YALE 10–3

SEVENTY THOUSAND WATCH TIGER TRIM

BULLDOG

DEVLIN SCORES ON YALE FUMBLE

There it was—not like the afternoon, muddled, un-certain, patchy and scrappy to the end, but nicely mounted now in the setting of the past:

PRINCETON, 10; YALE, 3.

Achievement was a curious thing, I thought. Dolly was largely responsible for that. I wondered if all things that screamed in the headlines were simply arbitrary accents. As if people should ask, 'What does it look like?'

'It looks most like a cat.'

'Well, then, let's call it a cat.'

My mind, brightened by the lights and the cheerful tumult, suddenly grasped the fact that all achievement was a placing of emphasis—a moulding of the confusion of life into form.

Josephine stopped in front of the New American Theatre, where her chauffeur met us and took the car. We were quite early, but a small buzz of excitement went up from the undergraduates waiting in the lobby— 'There's Dolly Harlan'—and as we moved towards the elevator several acquaintances came up to shake his hand. Apparently oblivious to these ceremonies, Miss Thorne caught my eye and smiled. I looked at her with curiosity; Josephine had imparted the rather surprising information that she was just sixteen years old. I suppose my return smile was rather patronizing, but instantly I realized that the fact could not be imposed on. In spite of all the warmth

and delicacy of her face, the figure that somehow reminded me of an exquisite, romanticized little ballerina,
there was a quality in her that was as hard as steel. She
had been brought up in Rome, Vienna and Madrid, with
flashes of Washington; her father was one of those
charming American diplomats who, with fine obstinacy,
try to re-create the Old World in their children by making
their education rather more royal than that of princes.
Miss Thorne was sophisticated. In spite of all the abandon
of American young people, sophistication is still a Conti-
nental monopoly.

We walked in upon a number in which a dozen chorus
girls in orange and black were racing wooden horses
against another dozen dressed in Yale blue. When the
lights went on, Dolly was recognized and some Princeton
students set up a clatter of approval with the little wooden
hammers given out for applause; he moved his chair un-
ostentatiously into a shadow.

Almost immediately a flushed and very miserable young
man appeared beside our table. In better form he would
have been extremely prepossessing; indeed, he flashed a
charming and dazzling smile at Dolly, as if requesting his
permission to speak to Miss Thorne.

Then he said: 'I thought you weren't coming to New
York to-night?'

'Hello, Carl.' She looked up at him coolly.

'Hullo, Vienna. That's just it; "Hello Vienna—Hello
Carl." But why? I thought you weren't coming to New
York to-night.'

Miss Thorne made no move to introduce the man, but
we were conscious of his somewhat raised voice.

'I thought you promised me you weren't coming.'

'I didn't expect to, child. I just left Boston this morning.'

'And who did you meet in Boston—the fascinating
Tunti?' he demanded.

'I didn't meet anyone, child.'

'Oh, yes, you did! You met the fascinating Tunti and

you discussed living on the Riviera.' She didn't answer.
'Why are you so dishonest, Vienna?' he went on. 'Why
did you tell me on the phone ——'

'I am not going to be lectured,' she said, her tone
changing suddenly. 'I told you if you took another drink
I was through with you. I'm a person of my word and
I'd be enormously happy if you went away.'

'Vienna!' he cried in a sinking, trembling voice.

At this point I got up and danced with Josephine. When
we came back there were people at the table—the men
to whom we were to hand over Josephine and Miss Thorne,
for I had allowed for Dolly being tired, and several others.
One of them was Al Ratoni, the composer, who, it
appeared, had been entertained at the embassy in Madrid.
Dolly Harlan had drawn his chair aside and was watching
the dancers. Just as the lights went down for a new
number a man came up out of the darkness and leaning
over Miss Thorne whispered in her ear. She started and
made a motion to rise, but he put his hand on her
shoulder and forced her down. They began to talk together
in low excited voices.

The tables were packed close at the old Frolic. There
was a man rejoining the party next to us and I couldn't
help hearing what he said:

'A young fellow just tried to kill himself down in the
wash room. He shot himself through the shoulder, but
they got the pistol away before——' A minute later his
voice again: 'Carl Sanderson, they said.'

When the number was over I looked around. Vienna
Thorne was staring very rigidly at Miss Lillian Lorraine,
who was rising towards the ceiling as an enormous telephone doll. The man who had leaned over Vienna was
gone and the others were obliviously unaware that anything had happened. I turned to Dolly and suggested that
he and I had better go, and after a glance at Vienna in
which reluctance, weariness and then resignation were
mingled, he consented. On the way to the hotel I told
Dolly what had happened.

'Just some souse,' he remarked after a moment's fatigued consideration. 'He probably tried to miss himself and get a little sympathy. I suppose those are the sort of things a really attractive girl is up against all the time.'

This wasn't my attitude. I could see that mussed white shirt front with very young blood pumping over it, but I didn't argue, and after a while Dolly said, 'I suppose that sounds brutal, but it seems a little soft and weak, doesn't it? Perhaps that's just the way I feel to-night.'

When Dolly undressed I saw that he was a mass of bruises, but he assured me that none of them would keep him awake. Then I told him why Miss Thorne hadn't mentioned the game and he woke up suddenly; the familiar glitter came back into his eyes.

'So that was it! I wondered. I thought maybe you'd told her not to say anything about it.'

Later, when the lights had been out half an hour, he suddenly said 'I see' in a loud clear voice. I don't know whether he was awake or asleep.

III

I've put down as well as I can everything I can remember about the first meeting between Dolly and Miss Vienna Thorne. Reading it over, it sounds casual and insignificant, but the evening lay in the shadow of the game and all that happened seemed like that. Vienna went back to Europe almost immediately and for fifteen months passed out of Dolly's life.

It was a good year—it still rings true in my memory as a good year. Sophomore year is the most dramatic at Princeton, just as junior year is at Yale. It's not only the elections to the upper-class clubs but also everyone's destiny begins to work itself out. You can tell pretty well who's going to come through, not only by their immediate success but by the way they survive failure. Life was very full for me. I made the board of the *Princetonian*, and our house burned down in Dayton, and I had a silly half-hour fist fight in the gymnasium with a man who later became one of my closest friends, and in March Dolly and I joined the upper-class club we'd always wanted to be in. I fell in love, too, but it would be an irrelevancy to tell about that here.

April came and the first real Princeton weather, the lazy green-and-gold afternoons and the bright thrilling nights haunted with the hour of senior singing. I was happy, and Dolly would have been happy except for the approach of another football season. He was playing base-ball, which excused him from spring practice, but the bands were beginning to play faintly in the distance. They rose to concert pitch during the summer, when he had to answer the question, 'Are you going back early for foot-ball?' a dozen times a day. On the fifteenth of September he was down in the dust and heat of late-summer Prince-ton, crawling over the ground on all fours, trotting through the old routine and turning himself into just the sort of specimen that I'd have given ten years of my life to be.

From first to last, he hated it, and never let down for a minute. He went into the Yale game that fall weighing a hundred and fifty-three pounds, though that wasn't the weight printed in the paper, and he and Joe McDonald were the only men who played all through that disastrous game. He could have been captain by lifting his finger— but that involves some stuff that I know confidentially and can't tell. His only horror was that by some chance he'd have to accept it! Two seasons! He didn't even talk about it now. He left the room or the club when the con-versation veered around to football. He stopped announc-ing to me that he 'wasn't going through that business any more.' This time it took the Christmas holidays to drive that unhappy look from his eyes.

Then at the New Year Miss Vienna Thorne came home from Madrid and in February a man named Case brought her down to the Senior Prom.

IV

She was even prettier than she had been before, softer, externally at least, and a tremendous success. People passing her on the street jerked their heads quickly to look at her—a frightened look, as if they realized that they had almost missed something. She was temporarily tired of European men, she told me, letting me gather that there had been some sort of unfortunate love affair. She was coming out in Washington next fall.

Vienna and Dolly. She disappeared with him for two hours the night of the club dances, and Harold Case was in despair. When they walked in again at midnight I thought they were the handsomest pair I saw. They were both shining with that peculiar luminosity that dark people sometimes have. Harold Case took one look at them and went proudly home.

Vienna came back a week later, solely to see Dolly. Late that evening I had occasion to go up to the deserted club for a book and they called me from the rear terrace, which opens out to the ghostly stadium and to an unpeopled sweep of night. It was an hour of thaw, with spring voices in the warm wind, and wherever there was light enough you could see drops glistening and falling. You could feel the cold melting out of the stars and the bare trees and shrubbery towards Stony Brook turning lush in the darkness.

They were sitting together on a wicker bench, full of themselves and romantic and happy.

'We had to tell someone about it,' they said.

'Now can I go?'

'No, Jeff,' they insisted; 'stay here and envy us. We're in the stage where we want someone to envy us. Do you think we're a good match?'

What could I say?

'Dolly's going to finish at Princeton next year,' Vienna went on, 'but we're going to announce it after the season in Washington in the autumn.'

I was vaguely relieved to find that it was going to be a long engagement.

'I approve of you, Jeff,' Vienna said. 'I want Dolly to have more friends like you. You're stimulating for him —you have ideas. I told Dolly he could probably find others like you if he looked around his class.'

Dolly and I both felt a little uncomfortable.

'She doesn't want me to be a Babbitt,' he said lightly.

'Dolly's perfect,' asserted Vienna. 'He's the most beautiful thing that ever lived, and you'll find I'm very good for him, Jeff. Already I've helped him make up his mind about one important thing.' I guessed what was coming. 'He's going to speak a little piece if they bother him about playing football next autumn, aren't you, child?'

'Oh, they won't bother me,' said Dolly uncomfortably. 'It isn't like that——'

'Well, they'll try to bully you into it, morally.'

'Oh no,' he objected. 'It isn't like that. Don't let's talk about it now, Vienna. It's such a swell night.'

Such a swell night! When I think of my own love passages at Princeton, I always summon up that night of Dolly's as if it had been I and not he who sat there with youth and hope and beauty in his arms.

Dolly's mother took a place on Ram's Point, Long Island, for the summer, and late in August I went East to visit him. Vienna had been there a week when I arrived, and my impressions were: first, that he was very much in love; and, second, that it was Vienna's party. All sorts of curious people used to drop in to see Vienna. I wouldn't mind them now—I'm more sophisticated—but then they seemed rather a blot on the summer. They were all slightly famous in one way or another, and it was up to you to find out how. There was a lot of talk, and especially there was much discussion of Vienna's personality. They thought I was dull, and most of them thought Dolly was dull. He was better in his line than any of them were in theirs, but his was the only speciality that wasn't mentioned. Still, I felt vaguely that I was being improved and I boasted about knowing most of those people in the ensuing year, and was annoyed when people failed to recognize their names.

The day before I left, Dolly turned his ankle playing tennis, and afterwards he joked about it to me rather sombrely.

'If I'd only broken it things would be so much easier. Just a quarter of an inch more bend and one of the bones would have snapped. By the way, look here.'

He tossed me a letter. It was a request that he report at Princeton for practice on September fifteenth and that meanwhile he begin getting himself in good condition.

'You're not going to play this fall?'

He shook his head.

'No. I'm not a child any more. I've played for two years and I want this year free. If I went through it again it'd be a piece of moral cowardice.'

'I'm not arguing, but—would you have taken this stand if it hadn't been for Vienna?'

'Of course I would. If I let myself be bullied into it I'd never be able to look myself in the face again.'

Two weeks later I got the following letter:

DEAR JEFF: When you read this you'll be somewhat surprised. I have, actually, this time, broken my ankle playing tennis. I can't even walk with crutches at present; it's on a chair in front of me swollen up and wrapped up as big as a house as I write. No one, not even Vienna, knows about our conversation on the same subject last summer and so let us both absolutely forget it. One thing, though—an ankle is a darn hard thing to break, though I never knew it before.

I feel happier than I have for years—no early-season practice, no sweat and suffer, a little discomfort and inconvenience, but free. I feel as if I've outwitted a whole lot of people, and it's nobody's business but that of your

Machiavellian (sic) friend,
DOLLY

P.S. You might as well tear up this letter.

It didn't sound like Dolly at all.

V

Once down in Princeton I asked Frank Kane—who sells
sporting goods on Nassau Street and can tell you offhand
the name of the scrub quarterback in 1901—what was the
matter with Bob Tatnall's team senior year.

'Injuries and tough luck,' he said. 'They wouldn't sweat
after the hard games. Take Joe McDonald, for instance,
All-American tackle the year before; he was slow and stale,
and he knew it and didn't care. It's a wonder Bill got
that outfit through the season at all.'

I sat in the stands with Dolly and watched them beat
Lehigh 3–0 and tie Bucknell by a fluke. The next week
we were trimmed 14–0 by Notre Dame. On the day of
the Notre Dame game Dolly was in Washington with
Vienna, but he was awfully curious about it when he came
back next day. He had all the sporting pages of all the
papers and he sat reading them and shaking his head.
Then he stuffed them suddenly into the wastepaper basket.

'This college is football crazy,' he announced. 'Do you
know that English teams don't even train for sports?'

I didn't enjoy Dolly so much in those days. It was
curious to see him with nothing to do. For the first time
in his life he hung around—around the room, around the
club, around casual groups—he who had always been
going somewhere with dynamic indolence. His passage
along a walk had once created groups—groups of class-
mates who wanted to walk with him, of under classmen
who followed with their eyes a moving shrine. He became
democratic, he mixed around, and it was somehow not
appropriate. He explained that he wanted to know more
men in his class.

But people wanted their idols a little above them, and
Dolly had been a sort of private and special idol. He began
to hate to be alone, and that, of course, was most apparent
to me. If I got up to go out and he didn't happen to be

writing a letter to Vienna, he'd ask 'Where are you going?'
in a rather alarmed way and make an excuse to limp
along with me.

'Are you glad you did it, Dolly?' I asked him suddenly
one day.

He looked at me with reproach behind the defiance in
his eyes.

'Of course I'm glad.'

'I wish you were in that back field, all the same.'

'It wouldn't matter a bit. This year's game's in the
Bowl. I'd probably be dropping kicks for them.'

The week of the Navy game he suddenly began going to
all the practices. He worried; that terrible sense of responsibility was at work. Once he had hated the mention
of football; now he thought and talked of nothing else.
The night before the Navy game I woke up several times
to find the lights burning brightly in his room.

We lost 7 to 3 on Navy's last-minute forward pass over
Devlin's head. After the first half Dolly left the stands
and sat down with the players on the field. When he joined
me afterwards his face was smudgy and dirty as if he had
been crying.

The game was in Baltimore that year. Dolly and I were
going to spend the night in Washington with Vienna, who
was giving a dance. We rode over there in an atmosphere
of sullen gloom and it was all I could do to keep him from
snapping out at two naval officers who were holding an
exultant post mortem in the seat behind.

The dance was what Vienna called her second coming-
out party. She was having only the people she liked, this
time, and these turned out to be chiefly importations from
New York. The musicians, the playwrights, the vague
supernumeraries of the arts, who had dropped in at
Dolly's house on Ram's Point, were here in force. But
Dolly, relieved of his obligations as host, made no clumsy
attempt to talk their language that night. He stood
moodily against the wall with some of that old air of
superiority that had first made me want to know him.

Afterwards, on my way to bed, I passed Vienna's sitting-room and she called me to come in. She and Dolly, both a little white, were sitting across the room from each other and there was tensity in the air.

'Sit down, Jeff,' said Vienna wearily. 'I want you to witness the collapse of a man into a schoolboy.' I sat down reluctantly. 'Dolly's changed his mind,' she said. 'He prefers football to me.'

'That's not it,' said Dolly stubbornly.

'I don't see the point,' I objected. 'Dolly can't possibly play.'

'But he thinks he can. Jeff, just in case you imagine I'm being pig-headed about it, I want to tell you a story. Three years ago, when we first came back to the United States, father put my young brother in school. One afternoon we all went out to see him play football. Just after the game started he was hurt, but father said, 'It's all right. He'll be up in a minute. It happens all the time.' But, Jeff, he never got up. He lay there, and finally they carried him off the field and put a blanket over him. Just as we got to him he died.'

She looked from one to the other of us and began to sob convulsively. Dolly went over, frowning, and put his arm around her shoulder.

'Oh, Dolly,' she cried, 'won't you do this for me—just this one little thing for me?'

He shook his head miserably. 'I tried, but I can't,' he said.

'It's my stuff, don't you understand, Vienna? People have got to do their stuff.'

Vienna had risen and was powdering her tears at a mirror; now she flashed around angrily.

'Then I've been labouring under a misapprehension when I supposed you felt about it much as I did.'

'Let's not go over all that. I'm tired of talking, Vienna; I'm tired of my own voice. It seems to me that no one I know does anything but talk any more.'

'Thanks. I suppose that's meant for me.'

'It seems to me your friends talk a great deal. I've never heard so much jabber as I've listened to to-night. Is the idea of actually doing anything repulsive to you, Vienna?'

'It depends upon whether it's worth doing.'

'Well, this is worth doing—to me.'

'I know your trouble, Dolly,' she said bitterly. 'You're weak and you want to be admired. This year you haven't had a lot of little boys following you around as if you were Jack Dempsey, and it almost breaks your heart. You want to get out in front of them all and make a show of yourself and hear the applause.'

He laughed shortly. 'If that's your idea of how a football player feels——'

'Have you made up your mind to play?' she interrupted.

'If I'm any use to them—yes.'

'Then I think we're both wasting our time.'

Her expression was ruthless, but Dolly refused to see that she was in earnest. When I got away he was still trying to make her 'be rational,' and next day on the train he said that Vienna had been 'a little nervous.' He was deeply in love with her, and he didn't dare think of losing her; but he was still in the grip of the sudden emotion that had decided him to play, and his confusion and exhaustion of mind made him believe vainly that everything was going to be all right. But I had seen that look on Vienna's face the night she talked with Mr Carl Sanderson at the Frolic two years before.

Dolly didn't get off the train at Princeton Junction, but continued on to New York. He went to two orthopaedic specialists and one of them arranged a bandage braced with a whole little fence of whalebones that he was to wear day and night. The probabilities were that it would snap at the first brisk encounter, but he could run on it and stand on it when he kicked. He went out on University Field in uniform the following afternoon.

His appearance was a small sensation. I was sitting in the stands watching practice with Harold Case and young Daisy Cary. She was just beginning to be famous then,

and I don't know whether she or Dolly attracted the
most attention. In those times it was still rather daring to
bring down a moving-picture actress; if that same young
lady went to Princeton to-day she would probably be met
at the station with a band.

Dolly limped around and everyone said, 'He's limping!'
He got under a punt and everyone said, 'He did that
pretty well!' The first team were laid off after the hard
Navy game and everyone watched Dolly all afternoon.
After practice I caught his eye and he came over and
shook hands. Daisy asked him if he'd like to be in a
football picture she was going to make. It was only conversation, but he looked at me with a dry smile.

When he came back to the room his ankle was swollen
up as big as a stove pipe, and next day he and Keene
fixed up an arrangement by which the bandage would be
loosened and tightened to fit its varying size. We called
it the balloon. The bone was nearly healed, but the little
bruised sinews were stretched out of place again every
day. He watched the Swarthmore game from the sidelines
and the following Monday he was in scrimmage with the
second team against the scrubs.

In the afternoons sometimes he wrote to Vienna. His
theory was that they were still engaged, but he tried not
to worry about it, and I think the very pain that kept
him awake at night was good for that. When the season
was over he would go and see.

We played Harvard and lost 7 to 3. Jack Devlin's
collar bone was broken and he was out for the season,
which made it almost sure that Dolly would play. Amid
the rumours and the fears of mid-November the news
aroused a spark of hope in an otherwise morbid under-
graduate body—hope out of all proportion to Dolly's
condition. He came back to the room the Thursday before
the game with his face drawn and tired.

'They're going to start me,' he said, 'and I'm going to be
back for punts. If they only knew——'

'Couldn't you tell Bill how you feel about that?'

He shook his head and I had a sudden suspicion that
he was punishing himself for his 'accident' last August.
He lay silently on the couch while I packed his suitcase
for the team train.

The actual day of the game was, as usual, like a dream
—unreal with its crowds of friends and relatives and the
inessential trappings of a gigantic show. The eleven little
men who ran out on the field at last were like bewitched
figures in another world, strange and infinitely romantic,
blurred by a throbbing mist of people and sound. One
aches with them intolerably, trembles with their excitement, but they have no traffic with us now, they are beyond
help, consecrated and unreachable—vaguely holy.

The field is rich and green, the preliminaries are over
and the teams trickle out into position. Head guards are
put on; each man claps his hands and breaks into a
lonely little dance. People are still talking around you,
arranging themselves, but you have fallen silent and your
eye wanders from man to man. There's Jack Whitehead,
a senior, at end; Joe McDonald, large and reassuring, at
tackle; Toole, a sophomore, at guard; Red Hopman,
centre; someone you can't identify at the other guard—
Bunker probably—he turns and you see his number—
Bunker; Bean Gile, looking unnaturally dignified and significant at the other tackle; Poae, another sophomore at
end. Back of them is Wash Sampson at quarter—imagine
how he feels! But he runs here and there on light feet,
speaking to this man and that, trying to communicate
his alertness and his confidence of success. Dolly Harlan
stands motionless, his hands on his hips, watching the
Yale kicker tee up the ball; near him is Captain Bob
Tatnall——

There's the whistle! The line of the Yale team sways
ponderously forward from its balance and a split second
afterwards comes the sound of the ball. The field streams
with running figures and the whole Bowl strains forward
as if thrown by the current of an electric chair.

Suppose we fumbled right away.

Tatnall catches it, goes back ten yards, is surrounded and blotted out of sight. Spears goes through centre for three. A short pass, Sampson to Tatnall, is completed, but for no gain. Harlan punts to Devereaux, who is downed in his tracks on the Yale forty-yard line.

Now we'll see what they've got.

It developed immediately that they had a great deal. Using an effective crisscross and a short pass over centre, they carried the ball fifty yards to the Princeton six-yard line, where they lost it on a fumble, recovered by Red Hopman. After a trade of punts, they began another push, this time to the fifteen-yard line, where, after four hair-raising forward passes, two of them batted down by Dolly, we got the ball on downs. But Yale was still fresh and strong, and with a third onslaught the weaker Princeton line began to give way. Just after the second quarter began Devereaux took the ball over for a touchdown and the half ended with Yale in possession of the ball on our ten-yard line. Score, Yale, 7; Princeton, 0.

We hadn't a chance. The team was playing above itself, better than it had played all year, but it wasn't enough. Save that it was the Yale game, when anything could happen, anything *had* happened, the atmosphere of gloom would have been deeper than it was, and in the cheering section you could cut it with a knife.

Early in the game Dolly Harlan had fumbled Devereaux's high punt, but recovered without gain; towards the end of the half another kick slipped through his fingers, but he scooped it up and, slipping past the end, went back twelve yards. Between halves he told Roper he couldn't seem to get under the ball, but they kept him there. His own kicks were carrying well and he was essential in the only backfield combination that could hope to score.

After the first play of the game he limped slightly, moving around as little as possible to conceal the fact. But I knew enough about football to see that he was in every play, starting at that rather slow pace of his and finishing with a quick side lunge that almost always took out his man. Not a single Yale forward pass was finished in his territory, but towards the end of the third quarter he dropped another kick—backed around in a confused little circle under it, lost it and recovered on the five-yard line just in time to avert a certain score. That made the third time, and I saw Ed Kimball throw off his blanket and begin to warm up on the sidelines.

Just at that point our luck began to change. From a kick formation, with Dolly set to punt from behind our goal, Howard Bement, who had gone in for Wash Sampson at quarter, took the ball through the centre of the line, got by the secondary defence and ran twenty-six yards before he was pulled down. Captain Tasker, of Yale, had gone out with a twisted knee, and Princeton began to pile plays through his substitute, between Bean Gile and Hopman, with George Spears and sometimes Bob Tatnall carrying the ball. We went up to the Yale forty-yard line, lost the ball on a fumble and recovered it on another as the third quarter ended. A wild ripple of enthusiasm ran through the Princeton stands. For the first time we had the ball in their territory with first down and the possibility of tying the score. You could hear the tenseness growing all around you in the intermission; it was reflected in the excited movements of the cheer leaders and the uncontrollable patches of sound that leaped out of the crowd, catching up voices here and there and swelling to an undisciplined roar.

I saw Kimball dash out on the field and report to the referee and I thought Dolly was through at last, and was glad, but it was Bob Tatnall who came out, sobbing, and brought the Princeton side cheering to its feet.

With the first play pandemonium broke loose and continued to the end of the game. At intervals it would swoon away to a plaintive humming; then it would rise to the intensity of wind and rain and thunder, and beat across the twilight from one side of the Bowl to the other like the agony of lost souls swinging across a gap in space.

The teams lined up on Yale's forty-one-yard line and

Spears immediately dashed off tackle for six yards. Again
he carried the ball—he was a wild unpopular Southerner
with inspired moments—going through the same hole for
five more and a first down. Dolly made two on a cross
buck and Spears was held at centre. It was third down,
with the ball on Yale's twenty-nine-yard line and eight to
go.

There was some confusion immediately behind me,
some pushing and some voices; a man was sick or had
fainted—I never discovered which. Then my view was
blocked for a minute by rising bodies and then everything
went definitely crazy. Substitutes were jumping around
down on the field, waving their blankets, the air was full
of hats, cushions, coats, and a deafening roar. Dolly
Harlan, who had scarcely carried the ball a dozen times
in his Princeton career, had picked up a long pass from
Kimball out of the air and, dragging a tackler, struggled
five yards to the Yale goal.

VI

Some time later the game was over. There was a bad
moment when Yale began another attack, but there was
no scoring and Bob Tatnall's eleven had redeemed a
mediocre season by tying a better Yale team. For us there
was the feel of victory about it, the exultation if not the
jubilance, and the Yale faces issuing from out the Bowl
wore the look of defeat. It would be a good year, after all
—a good fight at the last, a tradition for next year's team.
Our class—those of us who cared—would go out from
Princeton without the taste of final defeat. The symbol
stood—such as it was; the banners blew proudly in the
wind. All that is childish? Find us something to fill the
niche of victory.

I waited for Dolly outside the dressing rooms until
almost everyone had come out; then, as he still lingered,
I went in. Someone had given him a little brandy, and
since he never drank much, it was swimming in his head.

'Have a chair, Jeff.' He smiled broadly and happily. 'Rubber! Tony! Get the distinguished guest a chair. He's an intellectual and he wants to interview one of the bone-headed athletes. Tony, this is Mr Deering. They've got everything in this funny Bowl but armchairs. I love this Bowl. I'm going to build here.'

He fell silent, thinking about all things happily. He was content. I persuaded him to dress—there were people waiting for us. Then he insisted on walking out upon the field, dark now, and feeling the crumbled turf with his shoe.

He picked up a divot from a cleat and let it drop, laughed, looked distracted for a minute, and turned away.

With Tad Davis, Daisy Cary and another girl, we drove to New York. He sat beside Daisy and was silly, charming and attractive. For the first time since I'd known him he talked about the game naturally, even with a touch of vanity.

'For two years I was pretty good and I was always mentioned at the bottom of the column as being among those who played. This year I dropped three punts and slowed up every play till Bob Tatnall kept yelling at me, 'I don't see why they won't take you out!' But a pass not even aimed at me fell in my arms and I'll be in the headlines to-morrow.'

He laughed. Somebody touched his foot; he winced and turned white.

'How did you hurt it?' Daisy asked. 'In football?'

'I hurt it last summer,' he said shortly.

'It must have been terrible to play on it.'

'It was.'

'I suppose you had to.'

'That's the way sometimes.'

They understood each other. They were both workers; sick or well, there were things that Daisy also had to do. She spoke of how, with a vile cold, she had had to fall into an open-air lagoon out in Hollywood the winter before.

'Six times—with a fever of a hundred and two. But the production was costing ten thousand dollars a day.'

'Couldn't they use a double?'

'They did whenever they could—I only fell in when it had to be done.'

She was eighteen and I compared her background of courage and independence and achievement, of politeness based upon realities of co-operation, with that of most society girls I had known. There was no way in which she wasn't inestimably their superior—if she had looked for a moment my way—but it was Dolly's shining velvet eyes that signalled to her own.

'Can't you go out with me to-night?' I heard her ask him.

He was sorry, but he had to refuse. Vienna was in New York; she was going to see him. I didn't know, and Dolly didn't know, whether there was to be a reconciliation or a good-bye.

When she dropped Dolly and me at the Ritz there was real regret, that lingering form of it, in both their eyes.

'There's a marvellous girl,' Dolly said. I agreed. 'I'm going up to see Vienna. Will you get a room for us at the Madison?'

So I left him. What happened between him and Vienna I don't know; he has never spoken about it to this day. But what happened later in the evening was brought to my attention by several surprised and even indignant witnesses to the event.

Dolly walked into the Ambassador Hotel about ten o'clock and went to the desk to ask for Miss Cary's room. There was a crowd around the desk, among them some Yale or Princeton undergraduates from the game. Several of them had been celebrating and evidently one of them knew Daisy and had tried to get her room by phone. Dolly was abstracted and he must have made his way through them in a somewhat brusque way and asked to be connected with Miss Cary.

One young man stepped back, looked at him unpleasantly and said, 'You seem to be in an awful hurry. Just who are you?'

There was one of those slight silent pauses and the people near the desk all turned to look. Something happened inside Dolly; he felt as if life had arranged his role to make possible this particular question—a question that now he had no choice but to answer. Still, there was silence. The small crowd waited.

'Why, I'm Dolly Harlan,' he said deliberately. 'What do you think of that?'

It was quite outrageous. There was a pause and then a sudden little flurry and chorus; 'Dolly Harlan! What? What did he say?'

The clerk had heard the name; he gave it as the phone was answered from Miss Cary's room.

'Mr Harlan's to go right up, please.'

Dolly turned away, alone with his achievement, taking it for once to his breast. He found suddenly that he would not have it long so intimately; the memory would outlive the triumph and even the triumph would outlive the glow in his heart that was best of all. Tall and straight, an image of victory and pride, he moved across the lobby, oblivious alike to the fate ahead of him or the small chatter behind.